The Antitruth

THE ANTITRUTH

BY

MICHAELANDRE MCCOY

BECKHAM HOUSE PUBLISHERS, INC.
P.O. BOX 8008, SILVER SPRING, MD 20907

Copyright (c) 1997, Michaelandre McCoy

All rights reserved. Printed in the U.S.A.

No part of this publication may be reproduced or transmitted in any form or by any means, electronic or mechanical, including photocopy, recording or any information storage and retrieval system now known or to be invented, without permission in writing from the publisher, except by a reviewer who wishes to quote brief passages in connection with a review written for inclusion in a magazine, newspaper or broadcast.

Published in the United States by
Beckham House Publishers, Inc.
P.O. Box 8008, Silver Spring, MD 20907

ISBN: 0-931761-47-6 paper

10987654321

*In loving memory of my father,
Joseph C. McCoy*

Acknowledgments

The author wishes to thank all of the people, including his philosophy instructors, who have encouraged him over the years.

Contents

1. Dreams 1
2. First Dream 7
3. Mind Games 21
4. Many Happy Returns 34
5. Resurrection 44
6. I Am Nothing 73
7. The Keeper of the Globe 84
8. Revelations (The Antitruth) 122
9. Drops 135
10. The Wish 144

The Antitruth

Chapter One

Dreams

There's a thin line between reality and dreams. The more one learns about oneself and the nature of one's own personal perspective on life, the thinner that line becomes.

Sleepwalkers are dreamers in motion. The line that divides their two worlds has become fragile, and it reminds us that dreams are only a different form of reality. They are real within themselves, and often only awakening allows us to escape the circumstances in which we find ourselves while we are dreaming. Conversely, it is the land of dreams that provides the haven or sanctuary that, albeit temporary, allows us to escape the problems, worries, and pressures of everyday living.

In our dreams we can overcome any obstacle. We can bring back the dead. We can relive the past, glimpse at the future and realize the seemingly impossible. All of the "no's" that confront us every day can be turned into yesses in our dreams. The companionship we long for while awake may be blissfully experienced while asleep.

I have often wondered if we are truly aware that we are dreaming, when in fact we are only dreaming. I believe that part of our brain is always aware and guards over us, keeping a watchful eye on our imaginations, which are allowed go unchecked by our sleeping rationality.

Scientists have said that a person who lives in a constant state of depression will usually opt for his or her dream world and spend many hours a day sleeping. My own experience would perhaps serve to substantiate this claim. There are times when life seems to carry out a vendetta against each of us, and we are disappointed at every turn. With every plan, we find that the one thing that we couldn't let happen, does. Important papers are misplaced, bills are received late, and our deposit is posted one day after our checks have bounced. Our cars break down on the way to important appointments or interviews.

If you believe that dreams are hard to believe, then take a better look at reality. For no reason, people hate, kill, lie, and cause others hours or perhaps days of discomfort or inconvenience. There is seemingly very little reason behind much of what we do.

Descartes once brilliantly stated *cogito ergo sum.* I think therefore I am. He immediately admitted, however, that knowing that one is thinking does not in any way lend reality of a substantial sort, to that which one is thinking about. That is to say, I dream therefore I am, is also a valid claim. But clearly, no one in his right mind would suggest that that which transpires in his dreams is real. After all, we can all tell reality from fantasy, can't we? Or can we? I am beginning, of late, to doubt that this is always possible. Paranoids, schizophrenics, and countless others among us create a reality of their own out of the so-called reality that those of us who are "sane" acknowledge as "real." Children believe in Santa Claus, the Easter Bunny, monsters in the closet, the boogie man, and fairy tales until they learn otherwise. The shock of learning the truth, after growing up believing a lie, is apparently not overtly devastating. After all, we have all survived learning the facts of life more than once.

What we *believe* to be true is slowly being recognized as just that, a belief, not fact. We only approximately know the truth about anything. Some things we believe verge on being totally factual, while other things we believe hedge on being totally false. The trouble is, we often do not know which is which, nor can we be sure that we are capable of fully understanding the *total* truth about anything.

Being human, we must shape the truth in such a way as to facilitate our understanding of it. We must often "warp" the truth, so that we can incorporate it within our already mature system of beliefs. It is often easier to bend the truth than to change one's long-held beliefs about the nature of the reality that we experience. There are some things that we refuse to believe, knowing that we have every reason to believe them, and no rational reason not to. While, on the other hand, we choose to believe things that we have no reason to believe, and every reason not to. I'll get to some of these things at a later time.

What am I getting at? I am trying to say that in the course of living from day to day, one does not take time out to question why one believes any given fact. One merely accepts that one does, and he is usually satisfied believing it without further contemplation.

Occasionally, one is confronted with an "antitruth" that is so clear and so evident that one cannot ignore it or wish it away. One must acknowledge the presence of the "antitruth," and one must deal with it as best one can.

In many cases, this "antitruth" answers questions that are left unanswered by the "truth" one currently believes. And the reason becomes very evident once one learns of the "antitruth."

Revelations will occur; the ignorant will blindly reject them, the foolish will too quickly accept them, and the strong will too quickly oppose them. The wise, however, will embrace them and attempt to understand them, not with unquestioning faith, but with a love for knowledge and an unquenchable desire for truth. The wise know that once fooled, a potentially wise man can never again be made to believe so easily. It is perhaps good to some degree to allow the skeptic in us all to question even the most obvious. Only fools know all the answers. Only the wise know the appropriate questions. I do not pretend to know which of the two I am. Perhaps we all belong to both categories, depending upon the circumstances in which we find ourselves.

I do not expect you to believe what I have to tell you. I ask only that you take my words into consideration.

They are not the words of a blasphemous madman but rather the words of one who, through dreams that do not seem like dreams, has confronted the "antitruth," and who now seeks to share those dreams with you.

I have never written a book before, nor do I expect to ever write another. I do not pretend to be a prophet or a sage of any sort. But I am aware that the prophets and sages of old believed that the truth was revealed to them through dreams.

The mind is still the most inexplicable and unexplored frontier. We can only guess at the true nature and limits of its capabilities. The mind has a will of its own, and it often takes us places we do not wish to go; it leads us into mischief, rationalizes our wrongs, and inhibits our desires. We do not so much control our minds as our minds control us. The mind has the power to take the truth of our experience and mangle it until it fits snugly into our framework of beliefs.

Is there any wonder why we disagree on so many things? Rationality and logic have little to do with what we choose to believe. The mind believes what it wants to believe unless we force it to be more receptive and teach it to be more flexible.

We must become masters over our minds instead of allowing them to enslave us. We must open our minds to new truths and unlock the shackles of self-imposed rationality. We must experience reality in a new light and allow the alternatives that confront us to take on a credibility of their own.

There is more to reality than meets the eye just as there is more reality to fantasy than meets the understanding. When we believe in dreams, when we learn that few things are impossible while many are improbable—when are willing to subject the antitruths to careful speculation and admit that what we have always believed may in reality be wrong—then, and only then, will prejudice, hatred, deceit, and the need to feel superior to others be overcome.

We are blinded by our culture and environment to the truth that is inherent in other cultures and societies. We have allowed ourselves to believe that because something has always been the accepted case, it must remain so. If for no longer than the time it takes for you to read these words, allow your mind the freedom it needs to comprehend and consider what I have to tell you. It may or may not approximate the truth. It may or may not be a revelation, but the alternative it suggests has irrevocably changed me and the way I view life, truth, and reality.

If I am to be despised or condemned for what I have to say, then so be it. What is important to me is that I say it and that someone else hears and understands what has been revealed to me through dreams, dreams that somehow reek of memories.

Chapter Two

First Dream

The dreams began several months ago, more or less. The time isn't really important because it is purely relative. What we call a lifetime is an instant in the life span of one who is immortal. It was several months ago when I dreamed that I had met one whose life span flirts with immortality, though he assured me that even death would someday die, only to be reborn again. Before I get ahead of myself, allow me to regress to what I remember to be the beginning of my dreams.

I remember standing alone, lost in thought, contemplating my future. I wasn't thinking any particularly deep thoughts, just some common everyday thoughts about my estranged girlfriend and what I'd do with my life now that I had graduated from college.

It is the curious way in which I remember many of the minor details of these special dreams that perplexes me most because I've never been one who five minutes after I awaken, could remember whether or not I had even been dreaming. In any case, seldom if ever do I remember anything about the dreams I had. But I remember these dreams, which causes me to wonder about the nature of the dreams themselves.

Anyway, there I was, parked on the side of the road, leaning back against my car, gazing inattentively at the stars and thinking benign thoughts, when a shooting star caught my attention. It came from high up on the left side of my field of vision, and it proceeded diagonally downward at an angle, until just before it disappeared below the horizon. Trouble is, it never disappeared. It stopped.

Now, I admittedly haven't seen many falling or shooting stars before, but out of the few I had seen, none had stopped.

I had just about convinced myself that I had lost track of the original falling star and had mistakenly fixed my sights on a stationary one. Just as I was about to look elsewhere, I noticed that the star seemed to pulsate ever so slightly and then slowly start to grow in size. Just my imagination, I thought, so I stared a bit more intently. Sure enough, the star was growing!

You know, there are times when you're looking right at something, but you're not seeing it for what it is; like one of those black and white pictures that seems to change, depending on whether you are focusing on the black parts or the white parts. Well, suddenly, somewhere in the back of my mind, something snapped, and I realized that the star wasn't growing, it was heading in my direction! It was rapidly approaching me. Being prone to panic instantly, although gracefully, I decided to get calmly back into my car and get the hell out of there! One slight problem: the car wouldn't start. It wouldn't even crank. Well, the last thing I was about to do was jump out of the car and run. With my luck, I'd run in the direction the damn thing was heading. So, like the brave and rational hero I am, I covered my head and laid down across the front seats, bracing myself for whatever. Whatever never came.

After what seemed to be an hour, but couldn't have been more than a few minutes, I opened my eyes. Nothing. I mean no sound, no bright light, no explosion, nothing.

I slowly raised myself up like some Soviet spy in an old "B" movie and sheepishly peered over the edge of the door on the passenger's side. Slowly sitting up, I opened the slits in my eyes a little wider and saw…nothing. It was gone. Whatever it was it had passed by and missed me.

I was whispering to myself because it seemed appropriate at the time. I was safe. My luck had finally come through. I'd live to tell my grandchildren about it.

With a sigh of relief, I sat up. Something said, "Look to your left." I did. I saw him. My heart jumped up into my throat. My teeth ground into each other, my hands gripped tightly to the steering wheel, and my foot slammed down on the accelerator. Unfortunately, the car was still off. Doing what any red-blooded American would do, I lost it! I instantly reached over and locked the door. By now he was within five or ten feet of the car. I hit the ignition. The car engine roared to life, and I jerked the gearshift into drive, pushed the accelerator to the floor, and the engine stalled. The damned engine just stopped, dead.

I tried to crank it again while cursing it with every obscene word I could think of. I pumped the pedal furiously, but nothing was working. It was then that I heard the door lock click open, and before I could reach it again, the door swung wide, and there, three feet away, not much more than at arms length, I sat eye to eye with something, or someone like I had never seen before.

Needless to say at this point, I'm not the bravest of individuals, but I absolutely refuse to believe that I fainted. I mean, whatever it was, it wasn't more than three and a half or four feet tall. My last thoughts, I distinctly remember were, this thing's got a fight on it's hands!

The next thing I remembered, after waking up, was a warm feeling and a gentle vibrating massage starting at my head and reaching all the way down to my toes. It was almost pitch black, and I slowly came to realize that I was inside something. Something that instantly made me think of a coffin. So this is death, I thought. Well, at least it's comfortable. Just then I heard a faint humming sound begin, and a thin string of light appeared to my left. As the beam of light grew wider, I saw lights of different colors appear against a backdrop of smooth metallic surfaces. The coffin was opening, and I was about to meet my captors.

I could already hear them mumbling between them. What they were saying was all but unintelligible, except once in a while I seemed to hear my name mentioned, so I readily assumed that I was the subject of their discussion.

By now the humming had stopped, and a whirring sound began as I was tilted forward from my reclining position into an upright position. Just before I reached a totally vertical posture, they came into view, standing in front of me. There were three of them. All relatively short, all bald, and all very pale, almost as if they were partly transparent.

I suddenly became aware of my heart pounding loudly and rapidly in my chest. This was wild. Like something out of Star Wars, or some other sci-fi flick. But by far, the most unbelievable thing was that it was happening to me. I mean, nothing ever happens to me. I've always been the one who arrives after the action has taken place, and everyone delights in telling me what I have just missed. I remember thinking that this must be some kind of dream. But there I was, awake and semi-rational. And there they were, just standing there, calmly staring at me, waiting for me to do something. I tried to speak. Out came this garbled string of sounds that made absolutely no sense, and didn't even vaguely resemble English. My tongue felt like a lead weight in my mouth.

They looked at each other for a couple of seconds, and then one of them, I think it was the one that scared the hell out of me, back at my car, took one or two steps forward and said, with a really strange accent, "You are our guest aboard our...spacecraft, and with time you will learn more about who we are. What is more important, for now, is your physical condition. Can you walk?"

That was a good question. I hadn't tried to as yet, and wasn't sure I should try to without their permission. I took one step forward out of the coffin, and proceeded to watch the floor rush up towards my face. I fell forward, but I never hit the floor. Instead, I felt myself held up at an awkward angle, with my head about two feet off the floor.

I sank slowly to my hands and knees, dizzy and nauseous. My head felt heavy and my neck felt like rubber, which prevented me from keeping my head from bobbing up and down and from side to side.

I must have looked funny, because I detected faint smiles on the slits in their faces that I assumed were their lips. I tried to shout, "What are you laughing at?" but all I spoke was gibberish.

Like before, I received an answer to my unintelligible utterance. "You," he said. "You do look quite...comical."

I felt stupid. Here I was, a somewhat literate young adult, talking baby talk to three overgrown babies. I was getting angry, due to my frustration and fear. I guess helplessness brings out a lot of the more undesirable traits we possess. I'd never felt this helpless before, and I wasn't enjoying it at all. "We understand," he said, though I had said nothing. "But even you would find yourself...amusing in this...predicament, if you could see yourself. Do not worry, it will pass quickly. I am Trr, and these are my...associates, Zwig and Gnar."

This time I tried to laugh, probably because I felt it was my only way of striking back. I realized that it was childish, but it was the best that I could do in my condition.

Trr spoke again. "So you find our...names funny. We thought that Mi-kal was strange sounding also. You see, it's all relative."

"I guess so," I said, this time noticing a vast improvement in my speech. "But who are you? Why did you bring me here?"

"You are not the firzt nor the lazt," Zwig said.

"We much have to share with you," added Gnar.

"As you can no doubt tell," said Trr, "my...associates do not speak English as well as I. That is why I have been chosen as the...spokesman. English is my...specialty. Gnar specializes in Oriental dialects, and Zwig, in the Germanic and Latin-based languages. However, all of us are able to communicate with anyone we so desire, through...thought transfer, which allows us to interpret and convey...meanings instead of words. In this way, understanding is enhanced, and confusion is...minimized. By the way, I wish to...apologize for subjecting you to a mind-thrust earlier, back at your…automobile, but I distinctly heard you…think along the lines of assaulting me, and I had no wish to harm you physically."

"A mind-thrust?" I asked. "What's that?" I was stalling, looking for a chance either to make a break for it or to knock the crap out of these three pygmies. "A mind-thrust is what I will have to…reacquaint you with should you…attempt to carry out your…intentions. Do not be…foolish, Mi-kal, we mean you no harm. If you will try to stand now, I am sure that you will find that you are…capable."

It was becoming quite obvious by now that these three could somehow tell what I was thinking. "That is…correct," said Trr, "it is what you commonly refer to as mental telepathy. E.S.P. as you sometimes call it. It is a far advanced means of communication, once mastered, over that of the spoken word. With thought transfer, one is able to communicate mental pictures, or…'mentographs' as I like to call them. In this way, one can *show* someone what one means, as well as tell them."

Just then, Trr turned towards Gnar and Zwig, nodded slightly, and turned back to face me as they departed.

"Well, tell me something, Trr," I said, sounding as skeptical as possible, "if you can hear what I'm thinking, why is it I can't hear what you say to them, or what they say to you?"

"There are two reasons…Mi-kal. The first reason being that we do not wish for you to hear us, nor would it be of value to you, because we usually communicate in our own native…language. Secondly, your brain is not properly trained to…receive thought transfers that are not directed at you. At this point in time, we are not even sure that you are even capable of mastering such…techniques."

"Are you insinuating that I'm stupid or something?" I asked tartly.

"No," he replied. "Only that you are ignorant."

With that last remark I stood up. I still wasn't convinced that I couldn't take this midget on. "Don't try," he said. I have no desire to prove my superiority over you, physically or mentally, with any display of force.

"The people of...Earth still have light-years to advance before you learn to curtail your...senseless displays of violence."

"I'm not sure I like being insulted, but neither am I sure I want to risk being resubjected to another...uh...."

"Mind-thrust?"

"Yes!" I answered the voice in my head. I couldn't help but smile at Trr. He smiled back.

"A 'mind-thrust, is similar to a physical blow, but it issues from the mind. To one such as yourself, who is virtually defenseless against a mental attack, it is a very useful...method of antiagression."

"How does it work?" I asked.

"Simple, really." Trr replied. "Your problem stems from your...misbelief that there is a separation between mind and body. This...fallacy is propagated by those so-called learned spiritualists in your given...scientific and religious circles. The truth of the matter is that...brain waves are just as physical as sound waves, electrical waves, or...ocean waves. Once this has been accepted, the rest follows naturally.

"Consider this; how is it that if the mind is an intangible thing, it is able to stimulate the body, which is a physical entity, to react to thoughts? Surely, that which cannot be touched, cannot 'touch' that which is touchable. If that which can be touched can be affected by something other than itself, that something, must in turn, be capable of being affected by that which can be touched, rendering it touchable also. Are you…following me, Mi-kal?"

"I think so." I answered.

"Very well then. If it is agreed that the mind can cause or create certain reactions in the body, so that arms move at will and speech is possible, then the mind is obviously something that can…'touch' the body.

"You appear…doubtful. Nevertheless, the mind operates in much the same way as your present day…computers, only with much greater complexity.

"Brain waves are physical entities that are transmitted via…nerve cells, to different parts of the body, which respond correctly we hope, to them.

"Earlier, due to the effect of the 'psychovideographer,' or 'dream machine' as I like to call it, your mind was…disenfranchised, temporarily, from its normal state of consciousness, in which it receives and sends messages from and to the body, and was…redirected into the 'dream machine' which made a memory tape and pre-programmed your subconscious with subliminal mind pacifiers."

"What the HELL are you talking about!" I violently interrupted. "Did you brainwash me or something?"

"No, Mi-kal. Remain calm. You will later understand what the effect of the 'dream machine' on you will be, when you attempt to recall this…encounter you are now having. It's influence is very subtle.

"I detect a basic…distrust on your part. It is to be expected. After all, you still do not understand who we are. You will, I promise you, with time.

"Now, if I may resume my explanation. The mind is a physical entity, which ceases to exist when the physical body…dies."

"I don't have to listen to this crap!" I insisted.

"No, you don't, Mi-kal, but you should. You are being confronted with an 'antitruth.' An antitruth is something that causes one to react negatively to it due to its assault upon one's system of predisposed beliefs. The antitruth makes…sense, and it is logically sound but is not readily accepted due to the necessity of ones willingness to reject previously held beliefs, in order to incorporate the antitruth into one's framework of…experience evaluation.

"I think I have temporarily lost you, Mi-kal, allow me to…slow down. One of the inherent problems with thinking in dialects is that one may, in fact, hinder communication if one begins to wander outside of the boundaries set forth by the limitations of the familiar vocabulary of one's communicative partners. What I mean by this is that one may indeed be speaking English, but by using words or phrases unfamiliar to the recipient of the message, one may not be actualizing communication, but rather, be fostering…confusion.

"Good. You understand. Let me know if I get…carried away again.

"An antitruth, simply put, is a new belief that sounds truer than the belief one already accepts as being true. It stands against the truth, but it is not a lie.

"The 'truth' is often a fragile creature who, like a chameleon, changes 'color' with the differing viewpoints of its adherents. The truth is only generally known by anyone. What you believe or 'know' to be true about yourself is different from that which anyone else believes or 'knows' to be true about you; but it goes one step further. The truth is not that which you believe about yourself, nor what others believe about you, but both, neither, and in addition to all beliefs anyone can or is capable of having about you. The truth also changes.

"You look...puzzled, Mi-kal. I will try to explain. The truth is that I am standing exactly four feet seven and three eighths inches away from you. Although you have not detected my movement, I am now exactly three inches closer. Now a foot closer, and now two feet closer, at which point, the relative distance between us has noticeably changed.

"It matters not whether or not you can explain the motion, only that the truth, that is, the distance between us, was at that point in time, relatively true. However, if I now make the same...observation, the facts I convey will be fallacious.

"If I had previously believed myself to be exactly four feet seven and three eighths inches away from you, but was not, then I would not have been lying to you, because I believed it to be true at the time. A lie occurs only when one has the intent to deceive or mislead another or oneself. Without that intent, any statement believed to be true is not a lie. I may not know the truth, but then I may not know that I do not know it. Are you...with me?"

"Somewhat," I answered.

"Very good then, Mi-kal. The truth then, lies independent of our beliefs. The truth is also a fluctuating inconsistent thing. Remember that always. Truth is not always determinable, and once one acquires what one believes to be truth, beware of the sanctification of that truth, for it may surely change with time. We can never know the true truth, only our...interpretation of it. Thus, when I say to you, to be open to the antitruths, do not accept them with impunity, but subject them to careful ...scrutiny.

"Now, when I tell you that brain or thought waves are physical entities, you need not believe me, at first. Merely ask yourself, if they are not, then why did you black out? I will tell you why.

"Am I boring you, Mi-kal? I do have a tendency to...ramble."

"No," I answered, "not really. But I'm not too sure I understood everything you said."

"You were not fully expected to. Very well, then; when you stepped out of the psychovideographer and fell forward, why did you not contact the floor?"

"I really don't know," I replied.

"Because we did not permit it. We...held you up with the same force I had previously used to ...knock you out. Surely you've heard of telekinesis, the ability to move objects with one's mind? You have. Well, then, you should have some idea how we could easily hold your body up.

"Your body is an object and is therefore subject to physical forces such as our minds. My body is likewise, an object, and therefore is subject to the forces of my own mind. This makes levitation possible. By the way, that is the method I previously used to approach you, without any apparent means of transport. Levitation, however, requires a great deal of concentration and is mentally exhausting over an extended period of time.

"There are those, of course, who are much more...proficient at it than I. The mind-thrust you received was related somewhat to the telekinetic and thought-transfer functions of the mind. By disrupting the mental processes that control your bodily functions, for a split second, by mentally assaulting them, I caused a temporary...short circuit of your biomentlectrical system.

"Once one has mastered, to some degree, the art of this kind of assault, one also learns how to defend oneself against it. Similarly, once one learns how to...read another's mind, one quickly learns how to keep one's mind from being read, by creating a sort of 'mind-block.'

"The true masters are able to block in their own thoughts, while allowing the thoughts of others into their consciousness, and vice versa: they can then block out the thoughts of others, while allowing their own thoughts to be heard."

"We admire your...martial artists for their primitive development of some mind-over-matter techniques. The mind is a very powerful...instrument. Unfortunately, for those of you on Earth, you still let your minds master you, instead of you mastering your minds..."

"What do you mean?" I asked defensively.

"I mean that, much in the same way lower animal forms, let instincts and habits dictate their behavior, so do you. The ability to be rational, analytical, and non-behaviorally driven beings, shows itself within you. But your basic distrust of each other, and of yourselves, prevents you from acquiring greater knowledge of your 'inner' self, due to your preoccupation with your exterior self.

"The cultivation of the mind's resources is the greatest achievement one can aspire to. The people of the Earth are currently becoming aware of this and are beginning to...research mental phenomena in earnest.

"We have noted an improvement, although minimal, on the part of your people, and this is part of the reason we have brought you here. We detected your presence in a state of apparent...contemplation as we passed, and we agreed that you would make as good a subject as any, given your...cooperation."

"My cooperation in what?" I asked.

"Your cooperation in some very simple experiments and tests. The rewards to you will be invaluable, and we...promise you you will not be harmed.

"At most, you may experience some minor discomfort, as you did when you first exited the dream machine."

"Exactly what does this dream machine do?" I questioned.

"It serves many different functions, some of which you will become familiar with, should you decide to cooperate." Trr answered.

"Do I have any choice?"

"Yes, Mi-kal, the...decision is yours alone to make. If you chose to...forgo this opportunity for self-enhancement, then you are free to leave."

I don't know whether I said yes of my own free will, or due to something that the dream machine had done to my mind while I was in it. I answered a bit too quickly for my own satisfaction, and for some reason, I had a sneaky suspicion that I had been preprogrammed to submit myself to more of this lunacy. Regardless of the reason, I had still said yes, and it was that decision that forever changed my life.

Chapter Three
Mind Games

I awoke in my own bed. Everything was just the same as it had been practically every morning when I wake up. I glanced at the clock radio beside my bed and saw that it was seven-fifteen. I usually wake up about this time, give or take ten minutes, turn over, and go back to sleep, or semi-sleep as I refer to it. I'm asleep, but I'm still vaguely aware of everything that takes place around me.

I still wake early every morning, due to a habit I picked up while attending college. Although I had nothing to get up for, now that I had graduated, no one ever told my brain, so, alarm or no alarm, I wake somewhere around daybreak.

The only noticeable difference this particular morning was that I woke up with the previous night's dream still fresh on my mind. As I said before, I almost never remember any of my dreams, and those that I do remember fade away in a matter of minutes.

For some strange reason, I felt too restless to go back to sleep, so I got up, put on my robe, and did something I almost never do; I fixed breakfast. Eggs over easy and two pieces of sausage that were rapidly going bad. Another day or two and they would get that slimy appearance.

Well, such are the trials and tribulations of bachelorhood.

The milk had expired too! It only had a faint spoiled taste to it, but I drank a little anyway. As I attempted to eat this quickly deteriorating hodgepodge of sausage and eggs, with not-so-burnt, but very hard toast and old jelly, my mind flashed back to my dream. It was so clear that it seemed as if it had been real. I guess the science fiction movies I'd seen over the past couple of years had finally turned my brain to "phantasmagorical" oatmeal because I couldn't stop thinking how real it all had seemed.

The rest of the day passed in the usual dull fashion. I listened to the radio. No reports of any flying saucers. I listened to a couple of albums, one by Stevie Wonder and the other by Earth Wind and Fire. I watched the soaps. Yes, I watch soap operas on occasion, but so what? Nothing new was happening of any importance, so I listened to the last one while I got dressed for work.

I worked for one of those fast food chains, making fast food. I'm not saying which one, unless they pay me to say it. I've never been much of a company man. My loyalty grows with the size of my paycheck, and at the time I sure wasn't making enough money to consider myself beholden to them in any way.

That night, I closed my station, clocked out, and stumbled through the parking lot to my car. I was a little more tired and sleepier than usual, and was anxious to get home, watch a little late-night TV, and go to sleep.

On the way home, my mind drifted back to the previous night's dream. That's the last thing I remember about being awake that night, because I obviously had skipped TV and gone straight to sleep.

While I was sleeping that night, I had my second dream. I dreamed that I was driving, but I didn't know where I was going. When I got there, and to this day I'm not sure where "there" was, I got out of the car and turned around to meet Trr, for the second time.

"Hello, Mi-kal, how are you...feeling tonight?"
"A little tired," I answered.
"Are you ready to begin?" he asked.
"As ready as I'll ever be," I replied.

I followed Trr around a small hill covered with trees, where his spacecraft waited. It wasn't much larger or higher than a semi-truck, and it appeared to be saucer-shaped. Naturally.

We walked up a ramp and into the craft. I couldn't help but be amazed by how much larger the craft seemed on the inside than it appeared on the outside. Near the opposite end stood the ominous dream machine. I remember wondering what affect, if any, it had had on me.

Trr interrupted my train of thought by asking me to please be seated on an odd-looking seat without a back, kind of u-shaped, which was built so that my arms rested on the top of the u.

The seat was surprisingly comfortable. In front of me was a round opaque-looking glass table, which was somehow lit from underneath, or maybe inside the glass. Maybe the table was the light itself. I couldn't tell.

If you looked very close, you could see what appeared to be thin lines or ridges, etched into the surface of the table, crisscrossing and proceeding in all directions. However, upon touching the surface, the table felt perfectly smooth.

"This table, as you call it, is actually a very precise and intricate 'vibramotational detector.'" You will better understand its...function during the first test.

"This," he said, placing a small object on the table, "is a device that is particularly sensitive to thought projections." The object looked like a furry white golf ball, about one and a half inches in diameter, and had some kind of illuminating device inside it. At least I imagined so, because it glowed ever so slightly.

I reached out for the object, and it rolled away from me, over to the opposite side of the table. I leaned forward, and it quickly skirted, not rolled, but skirted over to my right. Using both hands to try to corral it, I grabbed at it, only to watch it jump above my hands, land on the table, and roll over to my left.

I looked over at Trr who was now accompanied by Zwig and Gnar. All three of them were smiling and trying not to snicker.

They looked like the Three Stooges, and I began to laugh out loud at them while they joined in their laughter at me. Now that they were distracted, I lunged for the ball and trapped it with both hands.

By now, they were laughing almost uncontrollably and only attempted to curtail their laughter when they noticed the annoyed expression I had on my face. I don't mind being laughed with, but I didn't like being laughed at! I felt like a trained chimpanzee or something. It was a degrading situation, and I attempted to reestablish a sense of dignity about myself.

Between subdued chuckles, Trr, Gnar, and Zwig apologized for their lack of couth, and we began to test in earnest.

The first test involved my futile attempts to move the ball by "thinking" it to move. It didn't budge. "Concentrate," Trr insisted. "You're not concentrating hard enough." So I concentrated. All I was getting out of this was a headache.

"You're going about this all wrong, Mi-kal. You are directing your…energy inward instead of outward. You must channel your thoughtwaves in the direction of the 'thoughtceptor,' like this."

The ball instantly began moving in an expanding spiraling motion on the table, until it rolled within a sixteenth of an inch or so around the edge of the table, and quickly spiraled inwardly, until it rested in the precise spot it had originally started from.

"What are you doing that I'm not?" I asked.

"The question may well be, what am I doing that you cannot, Mi-kal, but that has yet to be…determined. Please place this on your head."

He handed me a furry-looking helmet, which looked like a larger cut-away version of the ball on the table. Hesitantly, I put it on.

"Now, with the…'thought intensifier' in place, try it again," Trr urged.

I tried. I *really* tried. But nothing was happening. "Relax, Mi-kal. You're trying too hard. Relax and think about what you want the receptor to do. Project your will into it.

"This isn't working at all. Try closing your eyes!"

I could tell that he was getting a little perturbed with me, but I really was doing the best I could, considering the fact that I didn't know what the hell I was supposed to be doing differently.

"Are you so…dense that you cannot even project the tiniest bit of thoughtricity? It's hopeless!" he said.

Now I was getting a little upset myself, and defensive on top of it all. "Well, what do you expect me to do?" I yelled.

"If you had a brain, I'd expect you to move the damned object on the table!" he countered.

"Well, screw you and this stupid experiment!" I retorted.

"A typical misanthropic response from a moron who can't even move a thought receptor," he laughed.

"To hell with you and your damned thoughtceptor too!" I shouted.

Simultaneously, the ball jumped up and flung itself across the room. All three of them began to applaud, and I began to blush (as difficult as that is for me to do).

"Did I do that?"

"Yes, Mi-kal, you did. I intentionally angered you to...inspire you to do it. People on Earth have not yet learned to direct their psychic energies and to tap into their inner resources unless they are ...emotionally traumatized.

"You can learn to do it without anger, but this takes months, perhaps even years, to accomplish. In your case, as in the case of the overwhelming majority of you, the end result may or may not be considered by you to be worth the effort. We feel that it is.

"Although you would never gain the...facility to move almost any object at will, you may be able to move small objects with a great deal of effort. The important thing is that once these channels are opened, and this function of your brain, and the brains of your...contemporaries, have grown more accustomed to this enterprise, the chance for greater achievements on the part of your...offspring will increase, with each generation, depending upon the degree to which the practice of telekinesis is adhered to."

"You mean, if I practiced this every day, not only could I learn to move objects, but my children would also inherit the ability?"

"To a minor degree, yes, Mi-kal. But only if they too practiced it. Thought transfer is also a...dominant trait that, once acquired, can be improved upon with practice. Like any difficult task, it takes practice to achieve any degree of...proficiency."

"Fascinating!" I exclaimed. "Are there any more tests?" I was eager to continue now that I had achieved favorable results.

"Yes, place your hands on the surface of the vibramotational detector. This device also has the capability of measuring the thoughtricity output of the subject. By directing your thought waves through your hands and into the...table, you will be able to detect a change in the light intensity it emits."

I squinted my eyes and concentrated intently on the table. Maybe it was my imagination, but the table appeared to glow just a little brighter and then return to normal.

"Not sufficient." said Trr. "You're still directing most of your energy *into* your brain, as you attempt to concentrate harder, rather than letting it flow outwardly, through your hands, and into the table."

As I listened to him describing the process, the table began to glow brighter than ever, but died again as soon as I turned my total attention back to the table and back to what I thought I was supposed to be doing.

"Would you like to experience a...strange phenomenon, Mi-kal?"

"Yeah, Trr, I'll give it a whirr." I kidded. He obviously missed my attempt at humor.

"To better demonstrate the physical properties of brain waves, I will first ask you to remove the ...helmet, because this would only serve to...accentuate the results, which should be...spectacular, at the very least."

I handed the helmet to Gnar and was handed in return a pair of banded dark goggles by Zwig. As I put the goggles on, I saw that the others were doing likewise, and I felt myself growing excited with anticipation.

"Place your hands back on the table." This time the command came from inside my head. "We are about to do an experiment, using you as a thought conductor. Do not be afraid. You will experience a warm sensation. Do not remove your hands from the table, however, because this will break the flow of energy through you, and cause a psyonic overload. Your mind would experience an assault of such...magnitude, that it would literally blow its biofuses, rendering you a...vegetable. Remember, no matter how you feel, keep both hands on the table. Good, I have received your...affirmation."

Instantly, I felt Trr's mind lock into my own, and the table began to glow intensely. I sat there awed and fascinated until Zwig's mind also locked into my own, sending shivers through my body, as the table glowed incredibly bright. I didn't like this at all. I could feel my brain begin to smoke and my palms begin to sweat.

I couldn't have been less ready for the additional onslaught of Gnar's mind lock, which almost made me tear my hands from the table and reach for my head. But I was paralyzed with fear. Afraid to go on, afraid to stop, and not knowing how.

The table's glow was so intense that my eyes burned furiously in my skull, and I slammed them shut to ward off the now blinding light. The room was lit up like the heart of the sun, with cool heat. I was losing consciousness, while fighting to hang on by the sheer determination derived from the source of my fear for the consequences.

It was like someone was drilling into my brain without an anesthetic. I screamed from the pain. The table glowed so brightly that the light seemed to show right through the pores of my skin. I was losing it. I couldn't hang on. The world turned bright white, and the last thing I remembered was grabbing my head with both hands, and screaming at the top of my lungs!

I sat up in bed in a cold sweat. It was pitch black in the room except for the light on my clock radio. The time read three forty-three. My teeth were still locked together, and I tried to force myself to relax.

I was thirsty as hell, and my head ached. I got up, took two aspirins, and sat on the living room couch, in nothing but my underwear, waiting for the perspiration to evaporate and for the shaking to subside.

It had all seemed so damned real. I looked outside and saw my car, parked in one of the usual spaces, backed in, the way I usually parked it. That was one hell of a nightmare. Not a recurring one, I'd hoped.

I had a ringing sensation in my ears, like a high-pitched chorus of voices all singing different songs, none of which was loud enough or clear enough to be understood.

I also had this warm sickly feeling in my stomach, which felt like it was slowly rising up to my throat. It was evident that I was about to be sick all over the carpet with yesterday's breakfast, so I stood up to walk to the bathroom. My knees gave, and I slumped to the floor, half sitting and half lying, dizzy, and increasingly feeling sicker. Out of nowhere, I got a bad case of the hiccups, which only made matters unbearable. I began to have the dry heaves, which evolved into a coughing fit, which brought tears to my eyes. I couldn't breathe, I couldn't see, I couldn't think, and once again I found myself slipping out of the conscious world and back into darkness.

My eyes flashed open. I had no way of knowing how long I'd been out. Everything began to come back into focus. My disorientation was dissipating, but to my disbelief, I found myself lying at a forty-five degree angle, looking out into the control room of the spacecraft. I was back in the dream machine looking out through the now-transparent lid.

Trr, Zwig, and Gnar were standing across the room with their backs to me. Instantly, they turned, and began to approach me.

As you can imagine, at this point I was thoroughly confused. I no longer had any idea as to what constituted reality and how it differed from dreams. Somehow, the two had become entangled, and I was left trying to convince myself that I had dreamed that I had a dream while I was still in the process of dreaming.

My growing apprehension at the sight of these alien scientists was understandable, and I made up what was left of my mind to suspend any and all "cooperation," in any manner or form. I owed it to myself. They were obviously toying with me and felt that I was expendable. Well, maybe I was, but I was all that I had, and I had to preserve what tiny bit of sanity I had left.

Once, in one of my psychology classes, I sat laughing out loud at the bewilderment and pain being experienced by a cat who was being literally shocked into jumping over a divider in an electrified cage. Now I understood what the cat was feeling. *Why am I here? Why are they doing this to me? What do they expect from me?*

I didn't understand what they wanted me to do, or what would be gained from torturing the hell out of me.

    I was tired. I was sick. I was sick and tired of being tired and sick, and I wanted out.

    As if on cue, the front of the dream machine slid away as I was tilted upright. Cautiously, I stepped out and steadfastly stood my ground before this terrible trio. They said nothing. We stood there staring at one another; me: angry and ready to incite a one-man riot; they: quiet, passive, and unobstructive.

    I walked past them towards the portal, which opened as I approached it. I walked slowly down the ramp, glancing repeatedly behind me. I couldn't believe they weren't trying to stop me. I opened the car door and sat down inside. Still no attempt was made to detain me. I closed the door, making myself a silent bet that the car wouldn't start. I lost. The car started with a little coaxing and continued to run when I shifted into drive.

    I pulled forward, turning the car into position, to turn around. As I did so, I heard Trr's voice softly speaking to me telepathically. "As you can see, Mi-kal, we will make no attempt to hinder your departure. We just want you to know that we have greatly appreciated your…assistance, and we feel that if we have insulted or misused you in any way, it was unintentional, and we would like to give you our deepest heartfelt…apologies."

    "Bull!" I thought back. "As far as I'm concerned you can kiss my…."

    "Very well then, Mi-kal," Trr interrupted," we only regret that we were not able to share more knowledge about ourselves, and our purpose, with you."

    "Yeah, but at the rate you're going, I won't have a brain left to understand any of it anyway! You clowns play a little too rough for me! Just keep your mind games to yourselves, and we'll all be better off!"

I received no reply as I drove off, taking care to watch where I was going so that I could find my way back later on, if I wanted to.

I woke up at daybreak, as usual, and forced myself to stagger into the bathroom where I was met by the reflection of a pale, bloodshot-eyed, unkempt individual who somehow vaguely resembled me. I'd never looked so bad in my life. There was a white film in my mouth and around my lips, which were chapped and craggy.

I reached into the medicine cabinet in hopes of finding a stray aspirin or two, but found none. Swallowing a pill has always been a traumatic experience for me, so I usually opt merely to wait out any headache that comes along, which is usually no more than two or three times a year. Well, this was the granddaddy of all headaches, at least a seven-pointer on the Richter scale.

Suddenly, I flashed on a brilliant idea. I figured there was no way I could look and feel this bad, unless some of what I had dreamed had actually happened. I mean, maybe it was more than just a dream. It was a curiosity that wasn't going to go away by itself, so I slowly convinced myself to satisfy it by indulging in a little detective work.

I quickly dressed for work because I had the early shift that day, and armed with my camera, and a lot of determination to discover the truth about my dreams, I jumped into my '73 Pinto and traced my dream path back to where I remembered my last encounter to have taken place.

I'll give you one guess what I found when I got there. You

guessed it. Nothing. Nothing but grass, trees, rocks, and tire tracks. I couldn't even be sure the tire tracks were my own, or that this was the right spot.

I took out my not-so-trusty camera and took a picture of the small clearing. I have one of those cheap models that develops the picture in about two minutes. Unfortunately, it was still pretty early in the morning, and the light wasn't very good yet. Even in perfect light my camera only takes fair pictures, but this picture came out dark, with a reddish tint to it, almost like it was overexposed. Maybe the film was no longer any good.

You couldn't even see the tire tracks in the picture, so, a little disheartened, disgusted, and disillusioned, I balled the picture up and threw it into a nearby bush.

I climbed back into my car, convinced that my dream was, in fact, just a dream, and that I was being a little unrealistic by trying to convince myself otherwise.

I drove to work lost in thought, still feeling the dull, aching throb inside my head.

Chapter Four

Many Happy Returns

It had been a week since my last dream, Nevertheless, the dreams had become somewhat of an obsession with me. I found myself distracted, constantly staring off into space, both at work and while attempting to watch television.

I've never believed in going to psychiatrists before, but I was suddenly beginning to give the idea some serious consideration. I had read that certain dreams often revealed, or were symptoms of, hidden anxieties. Maybe some professional help wouldn't be such a bad idea, if I could afford it, which I doubted.

I'd been losing weight and sleep for the past week, with seemingly no coherent reasons why. Some of my coworkers attributed it to my recent separation from my girlfriend. I knew that wasn't the real reason, but I wasn't sure what was. Maybe, I reasoned, just maybe it was directly related to those dreams.

It was thoughts similar to these that I carried to bed with me that night. The night I had the third dream.

"It's good to see you again, Mi-kal." It was Trr's voice behind me. "We weren't sure you would ever return."

"Yeah, I just bet you weren't," I remarked.

"How have you been feeling lately?" he asked.

"Overall, on a scale from one to ten, about two and a half," I answered.

"Probably a side effect of the experiments you underwent on your last visit, Mi-kal. The effects could have been...minimized, had you remained in the dream machine a while longer. If you'll accompany me now, we can correct the...imbalances in a minimal amount of time."

I followed Trr to the spacecraft and entered once again into its now-familiar interior, where I was politely greeted by Gnar's voice.

"You are welcome back, Mi-kal."

"Yez, we have mizzed you," Zwig added. "We are glad you have reconzidered. We meant you no harm, when we lazt zaw you," he continued.

"Will you our apologies accept?" asked Gnar.

"Let's just say I'm not about to forget what happened, and that I won't be stupid enough to trust you three again with any more of your dumb experiments," I said spitefully.

Zwig and Gnar simultaneously looked at Trr, nodded, and set off in different directions to perform some unknown chores.

"Are you ready to enter the dream machine, Mi-kal?" asked Trr. Turning and looking him in the eye, I nodded, mocking his companions.

As I stepped into the dream machine and leaned back, I realized that this was the first time I had willingly subjected myself to its unknown influences. As the transparent dome-like cover slid around into place, I heard and felt myself being tilted into a reclining position, somewhere halfway between lying and standing. Just then the lid began growing dark and the outside world slowly disappeared.

My apprehensions must have been obvious, because Trr's voice popped into my head, reassuring me that everything would be fine.

Still somewhat skeptical, I tried to relax. An eerie feeling began to overcome me, and I felt as if I were suddenly floating, unaided and untouched, within the confines of the cylinder. A sense of well-being almost immediately swept over me, and I had the weird sensation of being back in my mother's womb.

The outside world ceased to exist for all practical purposes, and I was thoroughly content and worry-free for what may have been the first time in my adult life. I floated there for what seemed like hours, without a care in the world, and with no desire to return to the other world that may or may not have still existed outside of my own private little heaven. I was free. My mind was free. I felt almost immortal and in total command of all of my senses and of every square inch of my being.

I was softly interrupted by the faint whirring noise and humming sound of the dream machine returning me to a standing position in front of a waiting, and smiling, Trr.

"Well, hello there," I said. "How long was I gone?"

"About five minutes, Earth time," Trr replied.

"But that's impossible! I feel as though I've just had a good night's sleep!"

"Such are the…wonders of the dream machine. It does so much in its seemingly inactive way," Trr said.

"Exactly what does the dream machine do?" I asked.

"It performs many functions, Mi-kal. A few you have become acquainted with, and many you have not. Do you feel any better?"

"I feel a heck of a lot better!" I answered enthusiastically.

Something way back in the back of my mind told me that something was wrong. Why was I suddenly feeling so chummy with this guy, when earlier I had felt so defensive towards him?

"Is this machine brainwashing me in some kind of way?"

"What was that?" Trr responded.

"I said...."

"Mi-kal, I think you would be...fascinated with some of the functions of the psychovideographer. It serves as a device that facilitates a form of...meditation that we practice. It reestablishes coherency, corrects various biomentlectrical imbalances, records mento-graphs, acts as an image or holographic projector, allows us to facilitate visual communication over very great distances, and serves many other intricate functions, as well.

"Would you like to...experience another of its many functions, Mi-kal?"

"Will it hurt?" I asked.

"Not at all. Just lean back and relax."

As I leaned back, the lid slid into place, and once again I was tilted backwards. As I watched the cover grow dark, I became aware of a subtle difference taking place. Immediately after subjecting me to pitch blackness, I was suddenly looking out at what I can only describe as nothingness. It wasn't light as we know light to be, and neither was it darkness. It was the absence of both. It was sheer nothingness, and for an instant I felt totally alone. This prompted fear within me. It was then that I heard Trr's voice inside my head. "Relax, Mi-kal, you have nothing to fear. No harm will come to you. What do you see?"

A scene came into focus. "I think I see trees and children." I said.

"There's no need to speak out loud, Mi-kal, I am receiving you. Do you...recognize any of the children?"

"No. I don't think so." I thought back.

"Look a little more carefully at the little boys. Do you recognize any of them now?"

"I'm not sure, Trr, but it doesn't make any sense. What is it I'm supposed to be looking at?" I asked.

"Open your mind, Mi-kal, and you will come to recognize that which you are observing." "Well, one of the little boys kind of looks like my older brother Joseph, but he couldn't be any older than five or six. Wait a minute! Joe just threw his hat up into the air, and it got stuck in one of the trees. Now he's standing there looking up and pointing, with his mouth open."

"Very good, Mi-kal. Does this scene appear familiar?"

"Yes, it does. I remember it really happened, years ago, when I was a little kid. Hold on a minute! That woman passing by looks like my mother, only a lot thinner. I think it was her."

"Mi-kal, what you are seeing is one of your own memories, which has been recorded and stored within the memory banks of the psychovideographer. We recorded this and thousands of other bits of 'mento-data' when we first brought you here after our...eventful first encounter."

"What do you mean, you recorded it? Who gave you the right?"

"The right?" Trr asked.

"Yeah, the permission to go poking around in my head, recording my private life!"

"I don't understand." Trr replied.

"I just bet you don't!" I snapped. "Let me out of this damned thing!"

"Calm down, Mi-kal. You people are so...sensitive. After all, who is going to see this besides us? To be honest with you, most of it is quite boring."

"Well, Trr, it may be boring to you, but it's my life, and I don't appreciate..."

"Hold on just a moment, Mi-kal. Why are you being so defensive? My own 'mentoglyphics' are recorded in there. Once you come to understand that your life merely parallels, and in many ways almost identically mimics, the lives of countless others before you, and countless yet to come, you will realize that, if you've seen one life, you've seen a million. Yours is not so special that the entire...universe is waiting anxiously to inflict their...voyeuristic desires upon you. To the contrary, you should be flattered that your life is now a part of recorded history. Now, would you like to see more of it, or do you wish to persist with your childish protestations?"

"If you think I'm going to apologize, Trr, I'm not. But anyway, while I'm here, go ahead and roll the tape."

"Very well, Mi-kal, relax and I'll speed up the mentographs so that you may re-experience some of your past experiences. This process can be...unequaled in its ability to allow one to become better acquainted with oneself."

Suddenly, the scene changed, maybe a dozen times or more. Although the scene changes were rapid, I had no problem taking them in.

I couldn't help but smile, watching some of the crazy and sometimes painful events pass once again before my eyes. I saw my little hand picking up a small iron I had been playing with in the hallway of what looked like an apartment complex. Unknown to me, my brother had plugged it in, and when I ran it across my other hand, I was not so pleasantly surprised by the sudden unexpected pain I felt.

I also saw the time the wind blew through the open window in the living room, pushing the curtains into my father's football trophy, causing it to fall off of the table and break. To this day I think my parents believe that I did it.

Some of the memories were very pleasant ones, filled with loving relationships, dances, first kisses, football games, and awards I'd received. Maybe Trr was right. It's nice to know that my memories may well outlive me, thanks to the dream machine. I couldn't help but wonder how it worked. Suddenly, the images dissipated. I was in darkness, and I watched as once again I was returned to the real world.

"I think you've seen enough for one day, Mi-kal," Trr said with a smile. "Would you like to know how it works?"

"You know I would," I replied.

"Avoiding any…technical explanations, I will try to give you some insight as to its operational…techniques.

"The psychovideographer, as one of its functions, is capable of recording, for playback purposes, brain waves and mentographs. Please hold your questions. It is believed, by many humans, as we understand it, that thoughts are intangibles. However, as I have previously explained, they are, in fact, physical entities.

"With the advent of…computer technology in your society, the concept of the microchip and some of its capabilities is now becoming common knowledge among the better-informed of your species.

"As you may know, information of various kinds can be stored and retrieved through the use of these chips. The brain, particularly the neocortex, is extremely adept at recreating or recalling past experiences, with some degree of distortion and lack of comprehension, images or memories, within the mind. These memories, therefore, are obviously bits of information, stored within the brain, for retrieval purposes.

"Without the memory process, intelligence would not be a by-product of thought. Some behavior patterns are based on previous experiences and other behavior patterns established and passed on by your...parents. Habits are behavior patterns formulated and established through past experiences. Desires, cravings, and other subconscious motivators are also the result of stored information, which influences decisions and future behavior.

"The retrievability of 'mento-data' collected in the brain is therefore essential to survival and is a natural and continuous occurrence.

"Stay with me, Mi-kal. It will all make sense momentarily.

"The psychovideographer, or dream machine, is able to tap into the...memory banks of the subject, decipher, decode, and single out clear images, such as sights and sounds, experienced on a given occasion, and to record these images, memories, or mentographs, like a...movie camera or tape recorder. It is then capable of reproducing the recorded phenomena."

"Yeah, Trr, but what I saw in there was much clearer than the memories I have in my head. Not only that, but if it's possible to do all that, why haven't our scientists been able to do it?"

"That's a good question, Mi-kal. One reason may be because they are not truly convinced that it is possible. Another is that they have not yet developed the means or technology to facilitate this process. They are on the right track, however. Machines such as your...lie detectors, CAT scanners, and electroencephalographs are all very primitive forms of brain wave monitoring devices. When your scientists learn to decipher, to some degree, what information, as scant as it may be at this point, that they are receiving, they will be one step closer to being able to record and reproduce accurately brain or thought wave activity in the forms of sights, sounds, tastes, smells, and tactile sensations.

"At the moment they are only capable of producing lines and their variations, on a screen or a piece of paper, but one day, in the distant future, they may be capable of building a more primitive form of the dream machine."

"Why more primitive? Why not even better?" I asked.

"Because your brains are not as well suited for receiving, comprehending, storing and...regurgitating or assimilating, experienced or contemplated phenomena, to the same magnitude or clarity, that our brains are. In other words, the machine cannot be developed to meet standards that exceed the comprehensibility of its designers and manufacturers. If by accident they were to accomplish such a feat, they would probably never realize what they had done, so the additional information would go unnoticed or misunderstood. There are already many devices in use in your society today, which are capable of considerably more applications than you are currently using them for."

"I guess you're right," I said dejectedly. "It's a fantastic machine, but what purpose does it serve, outside of entertainment?"

"Think about it for a moment, Mi-kal. We have all but completely eradicated any occurrence whatsoever of criminal behavior in our society. How? Because those accused of a crime must agree to...stand trial, as you would say, by submitting themselves to the auspices of an even more precise and probing version of the psychovideographer. While inside, it is impossible to lie without betraying oneself, and one's actions during the committal of the crime can be easily recalled, retraced, and observed by the council.

"For this reason, improprieties occur about once or twice an Earth year, and the guilty party is justly reprimanded and required to make full compensation and restitution for his crime."

"Talk about something we could use on Earth! Tell me, Trr, if that's what you use it for where you come from, why do you have one here on Earth? Is it just to record the past of the people you examine, or is there some other use?"

"Our main reasons for having it aboard our spacecraft are now twofold, although at one time we used it for other purposes that I shall tell you about later. The secondary function for which we now employ it is, as you said, to keep abreast of the...maturation of Earth's societies, through the collection of mento-data concerning life experience in your changing and evolving world.

"Through the use of this information, and that which we ourselves add to the memory banks of the dream machine, we are able to affect its primary function here on Earth. That function is to record as unobstructively and as uninfluentially as possible the history of events on Earth. Our reasons behind this will be divulged at a future time. For now I think you've learned enough, and I must bring an end to this...visit. I will see you on your next return. Good night."

Chapter Five

Resurrection

"Good morning, Mi-kal." The sound of Trr's voice brought me out of a very restful sleep.

"How are you feeling this morning?"

"Better than I have for years," I answered.

"Excellent, then perhaps you won't object to continuing the conversation that concluded your last...visit?"

I looked around the room and found that I was lying on a flat table, which extended out from a slot in the wall of the spacecraft.

When I stood up, the table began to retract back into the wall, curving upward, inside the contoured wall's inner storage space. The end of the table, as it was pulled into place, filled the opening of the slot perfectly. The seam was almost invisible to the naked eye. I quickly realized that the walls, ceiling, and floor of the spacecraft, most likely contained numerous other devices of which I was totally unaware.

I yawned and stretched my arms outwardly, marveling at how great I felt. Still stretching, I glanced over at Trr, who was standing to my left, and out of the corner of my eye, I noticed a strange redness on the inside of my upper left arm, beginning about six inches above my elbow and reaching almost up to my armpit. I had to twist the skin around in order to really get a good look at it. It almost looked like a rash, but I wasn't sure. Maybe the redness was just the result of my sleeping on that side the night before.

"Are you hungry, Mi-kal?" Trr asked, interrupting my thoughts.

"Yes, I am a little hungry. What's for breakfast?" I asked jokingly.

"Take this. I think you'll find it satisfactory," Trr replied. With that he handed me a large pill. Trouble was, it must have been a good inch and a half in diameter, and about a quarter of an inch thick.

"What is it?" I asked incredulously.

"Nourishment," Trr answered. "It contains all of the necessary nutritional requirements."

"Trr, if you think, for one moment, that I'm going to swallow something this big, you're crazier than you look!" I told him sarcastically. "Besides the fact that you didn't give me anything to wash it down with, I can't even swallow a normal-sized pill. I wouldn't even dream of trying to swallow this horse medicine!"

"Mi-kal, as usual, you have…jumped to an inaccurate conclusion. You will not be required to swallow it, just place it in your mouth. It won't hurt you. Surely, if we intended to do you harm, we would have done it long before now."

"Sorry, Trr, but I guess I'm just afraid you're going to use me for a guinea pig again."

"I understand," he responded.

Hesitantly, I closed my eyes, held my breath, and put the pill into my mouth. To my surprise, it instantly began to dissolve. I can't really describe the taste, because there isn't anything I can think of to compare it with. It was delicious, though. Then, something strange happened. My mouth felt as if it had just taken a sip of some kind of juice. Then a third taste appeared, almost as good as the first, but different. It was followed by another sip of the liquid, and then by another taste of the original flavor.

This went on for about five minutes. One new taste was introduced near the end, followed by one last gulp of the juice. I was totally awed by the experience, and had I not felt full, I would have asked Trr for another one.

"Did you enjoy your…breakfast, Mi-kal?"

"It was delicious," I answered.

"I was sure you would like it. The nouri-tablet is one of our most widely appreciated developments. It has single-handedly all but totally eliminated waste, the destruction and dependence upon our environment, the slaughter of other life forms, and the problems of disposing of body wastes. Our digestive tracts totally absorb the nouri-tablet's contents, from which we find sustenance, and all of the energy requirements of our bodily functions. They are completely…inorganic and synthetically produced. They retain their effectiveness almost indefinitely and are easily stored and class identifiable via color."

"Yeah, and you've managed to make them taste pretty good, too," I added.

"Yes, Mi-kal. It is my understanding, that when first developed, several thousand Earth years ago, they lacked a suitable flavor, and the enjoyment quotient was further reduced by the rapid dispersal of its contents. As you can see, we also enjoy a good meal."

"Now that you have rested and…nourished, I believe you had

some questions you wished to ask."

"Yes, I did. Starting with, why did you keep me here last night?" I asked.

"In order to continue our...discussion," Trr responded.

"Are you sure it wasn't for some other reason? Did you use me for any more of your tests last night?" I asked accusingly. Trr didn't respond. "That's it, isn't it?" I asked irritatedly.

"You'll just have to learn to trust us more, Mi-kal. You have not been harmed. Please continue with your queries concerning our prior discussion."

"Okay, who are you, where do you come from, and what do you want from me?" I asked with growing irritation.

"Please make some attempt to control your emotions, Mi-kal. This is, after all, a...voluntary exchange of information.

"Now, first of all, it would make little or no difference for me to attempt to explain who I am and where I am from, unless you have a rather extensive knowledge of the surrounding...galaxies. Suffice it to say, for now, that we are friends, not foes. The greatest enemies you people of Earth must fear is yourselves. May I add that my...people have developed a growing concern for your...irrational outbursts of aggressive behavior. It is to your benefit that space flight on Earth is still in its infancy, along with the immature emotional and intellectual development of Earth's inhabitants. You need not fear our potential for aggression but your own increasing inclination towards self-destruction. I hope I have made myself clear!"

"You have, Trr. I'm sorry."

"Your apology is accepted, but further understand our position as well as your own. Earth is all but insignificant on a cosmic scale. Earth is but one of hundreds of known life-bearing...spheres in the universe, many of which possess societies equal to or far advanced of your own.

"At this juncture in the universe's known temporal history, the greatest, if not sole, significant impact on cosmic events the Earth and its inhabitants potentially possess is the dubious ability, using your primitive nuclear achievements, to blow the Earth out of its orbit and send it crashing into another sphere. This perhaps would cause a minor ripple in the spatial framework of your galaxy, but it would hardly be negligible or significant on a cosmic or universal scale.

"The Earth is only a single tree in the vast forests of the cosmos, and were its fruits to perish, none would be the worse but those fruits themselves. However, let us hope that as Earth's technologies mature, so does the nature of its inhabitants. Otherwise, self-preservation may incite some other species to terminate life on Earth for the welfare of its own."

"Okay, okay! You've made your point. Get off my case, already. I haven't done anything!" I said defensively.

"No, you haven't, Mi-kal, but often, there are many victims who suffer from the insane act of one. On Earth, the majority suffer so that the few may thrive on riches and power."

"Isn't it the same on your planet, Trr?"

"It was a million or so Earth years ago. About a thousand years before the Resurrection," Trr said wistfully.

"What was the Resurrection?" I asked

"The Resurrection, Mi-kal, was, for the most part, a reevaluation of our ideals, our aspirations, our collective goals, and our self-identity. The Resurrection was the end result of our own technology outgrowing our social and spiritual maturity. To our benefit, however, our science was able to save us after it had all but destroyed us."

"What changes did you have to make, and why couldn't you have made them before it all went wrong?" I asked.

"Unfortunately, maturity and rationality are often the result of catastrophe. It is easy to look back now and see how we could have easily avoided the massive deterioration of our cities, morals, and, ultimately, our way of life. When the preservation of life and the quality of life become anything less than the first priority of a given society, that society will destroy itself from within.

"We scoffed at traditions, defended, and provided for and supported antisocial behaviorists, and ultimately glorified science, technology, and achievement at the expense of ethics, morals, and responsibility. In a sense, we outsmarted ourselves.

"When a society places its emphasis on life-destroying, rather than life-enhancing, technology, then it is only a matter of time before it uses those forces to its own disadvantage. In other words, if you have a gun, sooner or later you'll find a reason to use it.

"One misplaced threat, one needless show of force, one weapon used in arrogance by a single misguided ego, and the seeds of chaos, destruction, and needless countless deaths may be sown."

"I know what you mean, Trr. We have the same type of problems threatening us here on Earth. One maniac could single-handedly bring an end to millions of lives with one rash act. How did your people avoid it?"

"We didn't," Trr said quietly.

"What do you mean, you didn't? If you didn't, you wouldn't be standing here now," I asserted.

"Remember, our technology was able to save some remnants of life from our...sphere. However, we were much further advanced, technologically, than you presently are on Earth.

"Our scientists had, supposedly, accurately determined the effects of...radiation levels, their duration of harmfulness, the parameters of the affected areas, alternative shelter and escape avenues, and survival quotients.

"All wrong. Their figures were all wrong. We believed them, and that belief all but completely destroyed us. You see, Mi-kal, we computed the effect our weapons would directly have on others of our species. What we failed to compute accurately was the full extent of their ecological, atmospheric, and psychological effects. Yet some of us survived our own brilliant strategists."

"How did you manage that, Trr?"

"The only survivors were some of those chosen to be on the evacuation contingency lists of the different 'factions.' These were hand-selected groups of approximately one hundred thousand each, only half of whom survived the journey to the nearest habitable planet. Of those that survived the exodus, about fifteen percent were later found to suffer from post-nuclear effects. Birth defects, including physical and mental disabilities, showed up in infants as much as three...generations later.

"The survivors of different factions, from all over our sphere, landed at different intervals and in different hemispheres on the new planet. The more militaristic of the survivors instantly began anew the fighting that had previously resulted in our near total demise. The wiser individuals of the differing factions formed the first...Assembly to discuss the growing problem. It was instantly agreed that all fighting must cease immediately.

"The military leaders disagreed, shouting slogans of faction pride, heritage, tradition, and patriotism. In perhaps the bloodiest confrontation in the history of my species, thousands of people died. In the end, the Assembly prevailed, and peace was realized, but only after the last of the military leaders yielded or were…terminated." Trr lowered his head and grew silent.

"You seem to still feel the pain of what happened, Trr. How long ago was it?"

"Over a million Earth years ago," he said sadly.

"And you still feel hurt by it?" I asked, amazed.

"Yes, Mi-kal. Although it was long before I…became, it is the shame my species endures. The post-nuclear effects still persist, you see."

"Yeah, I guess I do. What happened after that?" I asked respectfully.

"Resurrection," he answered. "Another Assembly was…selected. They unanimously agreed that all previous factions should unite, due to the devastation of our numbers, and rebuild one society, together.

"About three hundred thousand survivors from all factions joined together in building a new city. A few…rebels from each faction that had somehow survived the…war remained on the outskirts, slowly diminishing their own ranks through brutal confrontations. Those that infiltrated the new city were captured and…eliminated.

"All of the schools were built with the same principles in mind. Maximize oneness, emphasize unity, deemphasize differences, and eradicate prejudices. This was accomplished by initiating a single new language that contained remnants of all of the elder dialects.

Cross-breeding of the factions was encouraged. Only one form of scientifically based creationism was taught and practiced.

"One…government was formed, consisting of a rotating assembly of elders, which ensured that no individual served longer than five of our years, consecutively, in the same capacity. One set of accepted behavioral practices became the basis of our…laws. All acceptable practices were based on the logic of mutual benefit. We believe that as part of a given…society, one is obligated to adhere to the basic mores and acceptable behavior patterns of that society. This means I agree that, should I take the life, in any manner which is deemed malicious, premeditated, or callous, of any other of my species, I in turn give the other members of my species, in that society, the right, no, the obligation, to take my own life in retribution."

"This also assures me that…justice will be dealt to those who may inflict harm against me. It is considered an unwritten agreement among all members of my species.

"Of course, there are exceptions, such as accidents, self-defense, and crimes of passion, which may lack prior contemplation, but these instances are all but unheard of. So, too, is antisocial behavior of any kind.

"In the first year of the Resurrection, freedom was discussed. My…ancestors understood the limitations that must be placed upon absolute freedom. One must be held accountable to the other individuals of one's society, otherwise, justice is an impossibility.

"We are free to engage in any act and in any criticism of our society, within the bounds of respect and the noninterference or nonsuppression of others. In other words, we retained the right to appear before an Assembly and express our ideas, concerns, and disagreements with current practices. Our suggestions and protests are heard and reviewed, and judgment is passed. We are obligated to adhere to the decision but not hindered from continuing to voice our own...personal points of view.

There are no boundaries, such as borderlines, fences, or restricted areas, within which a citizen cannot enter. The only exception to this is that of the private dwelling. Each...'post-pupil' who desires an independent private dwelling is granted one. No one, without the legal consent on the part of the Assembly, may enter into a private dwelling, without the direct consent of the resident. Dwellings cannot be confiscated for any reason but can be surrendered by the resident, at any time he or she chooses. This usually occurs when a...companion is taken, co-occupancy is desired, or a petition for relocation is granted.

"Every post-pupil is guaranteed employment on a level that he or she is suited for. Every post-pupil that can work is required to do so. However, one may advance in one's occupation when desired, provided an opening is available, and one has acquired the...training and education to perform in the desired position capably.

"Performance is emphasized for the benefit of the whole. Unless one acquires the advanced skills and training, such as those requirements needed to become a 'Witnesser,' like myself, the beginning, less-specialized occupations are delegated on a rotating basis. Each year, on our sphere, there is a shift of responsibilities. Everyone takes his or her turn in the fields of nourishment development, dwelling maintenance, communication enhancement, and many other areas of societal concerns. This eliminates boredom and class evolution."

"Excuse me, Trr, but your idea of limited freedom sounds *extremely* limited to me. How can you limit freedom, and still be free?"

"Freedom, Mi-kal, is an...illusion. Your society seems to harbor the idea that freedom is an either/or state of being. That is to say either one is free or one is not. The truth of the matter is that there is nothing in the universe that enjoys complete or total freedom. I will explain.

"Inherent in being is the presupposition that for anything to be, it must *be* something. Once that something is defined, its limitations become evident. Absolute freedom would suggest the capacity to become whatever one desires to be, regardless of what one is. It also entails the capacity to do or to cause anything one wishes to occur. Unfortunately, the study of universal physics, has shown us that existence is irrevocably tied to essences, and that although there are various species and materials composed of undefined or unstable...substances, even they are limited by the nature of their own compositions.

"There will always be limitations as to how fast, how large, how small, how hot, how cold, how constant, or how temporal, among many other determinate factors, any single entity may become. All of these reasons contribute to a reduction of freedom."

"Trr, what are you talking about?" I interrupted "What has any of that nonsense got to do with whether or not I'm free to do whatever I want, go wherever I want, or think and say whatever I want?"

"If I may continue, I will attempt to clarify," Trr responded. "first of all, you are free to do only that which you are capable of doing. For instance, you are not free to fly, without the aid of some artificial flying device. Most birds share this freedom, but they are limited by how fast, how high, and how far they may exercise that freedom. As a...human being, you are incapable of breathing underwater, but a fish has no such limitation. The fish is, on the other hand, not free to walk on land, as you do. So you see, you are only free to do that which you, as a human being on Earth, are capable of doing, however limited that may be.

"So long as you do not aspire to do that which you cannot, you are free to do whatever you want. If one were confined to a room and possessed no desire to leave that room, or to experience anything outside of that room, then being forcibly removed from the room and released into the outside world would be an infringement upon one's freedom to do what one wanted. On the other hand, if one wishes to leave the room but cannot, one's freedom is equally hampered.

"Freedom, Mi-kal, is best defined as the ability to do that which one is capable of doing when one desires to do it. The parameters of one's actions, however, are limited to the capabilities one possesses. A goldfish that wants nothing more out of life than to swim around in an aquarium is free, whereas, should you desire to walk to the moon, your lack of freedom to do so becomes obvious. That is the illusion of freedom; it is defined by its limitations. You are free to speak so long as you are capable, but you are limited to speaking your native tongue, unless you expand your limitations by learning other languages.

"You are also limited by others. One learns that what one says often carries with it the consequences of saying it, whether or not one wishes to face those consequences.

"Therefore, if one is spanked as a child, or later punished by the law, for what one has said publicly or privately, in the presence of others, one learns that one's freedom of speech carries with it responsibility and is limited by the reprisals of others who may not wish to hear it.

"Therefore, if one wishes to say something, but does not wish to suffer the consequences of having said it, one's freedom is infringed upon by the consequences of the act itself. This also extends to one's actions. Have I made myself understood?"

"Yes, but I'm still free to think it, right? I mean, I'm free to think anything I want to think, and there aren't any consequences that will result due merely to my thinking something to myself," I stated confidently.

"Not necessarily, Mi-kal. For one thing, what one thinks has an effect on ones respiration, heartbeat, and many other biomentlectrical systems. I believe you have a saying: 'Healthy mind, healthy body.' It is truer than one supposes. Many illnesses are psychosomatically induced, such as heart attacks, ulcers, migraine headaches, and other stress-related dysfunctions. Furthermore, my species is capable of monitoring...thought patterns. Therefore, unless we consciously induce a mind-block, others of my species are capable of...hearing what the other is thinking, just as if it were spoken out loud. One last point. You are only free to think thoughts that are the direct or indirect result of your experience. Even that which one imagines is nothing more than a combination of elements previously experienced."

"What do you mean? I think of things that I'm sure no one else has thought of in exactly the same way that I have," I asserted.

"Another 'fact' that is merely presupposition on your part.

Though it may be questionably possible for you to think of something that no one before you has ever thought, nevertheless, you and I are incapable of thinking something that is not either a combination of previous thoughts or experiences, or a compound of principles, theories, and concepts, previously based on our experiences.

"One uses concepts such as 'infinite,' to describe things that are uncountable. However, something is not infinite simply because we cannot count it. How, then, could there be an infinite number of grains of sand on a beach if the beach itself has limitations. So, too, how can there be an infinite number of stars and spheres in the universe? Infinity is a concept that is defined in such a way as to appease our understanding, but infinity itself cannot be comprehended.

"The concept of infinity stems from the synthesis of experienced, countable phenomena and mathematics, which is the symbolic and implied relationship between that which we have experienced and that which we cannot. I defy you to come up with a number which has no practical application. All numbers and their relationship to one another, stem from our attempt to understand our experiences and to communicate them to others. If such a number were derived that could not be practically applied or communicated, then we would not have a number, merely a word, and possibly not even that if the word itself has no meaning.

"The term or concept of 'eternal,' likewise, merely expresses our inability to measure the duration of something. The concept itself is meaningless, except to express the fact that our thinking is limited to rational undertakings, for in reality, there is nothing that we have been made aware of, that is eternal, everlasting, or endless in the universe. We understand what is implied by the terms, but we are incapable of conceptualizing the applicability of these terms to any experiential phenomena. One may assert that one understands the implications of the word, but not that one can picture it in one's mind, nor is one capable of experiencing it.

"I don't expect you to accept what I have attempted to covey to you, Mi-kal, so consider it an 'antitruth.' That is all that I can ask of you for now."

"I think I understood you, but I still think I know what it means to be infinite and eternal. I almost believe you about not being able to think of something totally different from anything I've ever seen, heard or thought. But whenever I attempt to describe it to myself, I use terms that already have meaning to me, such as, it has wings, or it's hot, or it travels so fast the eye can't see it. No matter how I try to think of something original, it's always a combination of things I already understand. One exception though, the nouri-tablet you gave me had an indescribable taste, but it probably tastes differently to me than it does to you. Would this qualify as an original thought?" I asked.

"No. Simply because your impressions of the nouri-tablet are contingent upon your experience of it. New experiences generate new ideas, comparisons, and relationships, but once again, they are the end result of experienced phenomena and therefore only derivations of the experience itself can be conceptualized. By this I mean, you may think of similar tastes which are a little more-so or a little less-so. Remember, and I stand firm on this, we are limited to thinking or conceptualizing only those things that are related to, resulting from, combinations of, or derivations of experienced phenomena."

"Okay, enough already. Tell me more about your social structure," I prodded.

"Very well then." Trr continued, "After ten or more complete social rotations, the post-pupil…"

"Wait a minute," I interrupted, "just what is a post-pupil?"

"A 'post-pupil,'" Trr explained, "is an individual who has completed the educational equivalent of three of your master's degrees in three different fields of study. Everyone is required, by law, to fulfill this sociological obligation, no matter how long it may take."

"And just how long does it usually take?" I asked.

"Most individuals finish by…Earth age thirty-five."

"Thirty-five!" I exclaimed.

"Yes, but to us this is a very young and rather immature state of…development. One believes, by this age, that one knows or understands much more than one actually does. As it is often said, a little knowledge can be a very dangerous commodity.

"After one's preliminary education has been completed, one enters the rotation."

"Excuse me again," I interrupted, "just how long do you people live anyway?"

Trr paused. He turned and glanced at Zwig and Gnar, who were monitoring screens on the other side of the room. They both nodded and turned back to their tasks.

"It depends," Trr answered.

"On what?" I insisted.

"On many factors," he replied.

"Like what?" I demanded. "How old are you?"

Reluctantly, Trr answered. "Close to one thousand of your

Earth years."

"What?" I yelled. "That's impossible!"

"There you go again, Mi-kal, making uninformed conclusions based on your own limited experiential data."

"Explain it, then," I prompted, "but I'm not sure I'm going to believe you this time."

"Mi-kal, you see the world, time, the universe, and life, as you must, given your point of reference. My species has developed technologies that have tremendously reduced the aging process. Our internal organs do less than half the work of your own, due to our advanced nutritional practices, regular organ enhancement, restructuring, and replacement. Instead of bowel movements, we take a 'purging pill' approximately once an Earth month, to remove any impurities we may have absorbed due to our interaction with the environment.

"Where I come from, stress has been all but completely eliminated, due to the reduction of uncertainty about one's life, direction, well-being and status. Those of us who become 'temporarily imbalanced,' voluntarily undergo psychological realignment, and if desired, sociological reassignment. You merely have to request it.

"Learning what to do, and not do, to our bodies and minds, is an ongoing area of development in our society. Nothing is taken for granted, and no desire is considered unimportant. This does not mean, however, that one may have anything one wants when one wants it, but through education, experience, and patience, some degree of self-satisfaction and fulfillment can be achieved in any area in which one chooses to excel.

"In other words, Mi-kal, because one knows that everything

one wants is just a matter of time and effort, one need not become frustrated, disillusioned, or 'stressed out' over its eventuality. While undergoing one's educational fulfillment requirement, one takes four to five years, off and on, of socialization and patience enhancement courses."

"Trr," I interjected, "you've made your point. Go on."

"As I was saying, Mi-kal, life's duration is affected by many contributing factors. By reducing or eliminating these factors, and by enhancing and promoting 'happiness or well-being' fulfillment practices, one can greatly extend life, through psychological, medical, and technological means.

"While...traveling to your sphere, the three of us placed ourselves in stasis, thus adding many chronological years to our life spans. At any rate, fifteen hundred earth years is not an unreasonable nor unattainable age limitation for us."

"How long did it take you to get here?" I asked.

Once again Trr turned to his companions. Quickly turning back to me, he replied, "I am not at liberty to disclose such information. Once again, your people are of no threat whatsoever to mine, but to reduce the chance of that likelihood, some information cannot be shared."

"Lighten up, Trr," I said, smiling. "It's nice to know I can make you nervous, too." Trr gave me a gentle smile in return. "Do you have any kids?" I continued. A strange look came over Trr's barely expressive face. "You know," I added, "children, offspring, like in sons and daughters..."

"I understand," Trr interrupted. "Mi-kal, there are some practices that are personally so incongruent with the vicissitudes of ones 'lifescope' that one hasn't considered the...likelihood or relative importance of a given enterprise."

"There you go again!" I said sarcastically.

"What I mean, Mi-kal, is that we do not give birth to offspring, the way your people do. We haven't for thousands and thousands of years."

"You mean you don't have parents? None of you?" I asked in disbelief. "That's got to be impossible!"

"You're right," Trr responded. "What I meant was that we do not give birth, or parent, the way you do. I may or may not have several offspring, while at the same time, all of our youth, including those one generation 'younger' than myself, may in fact, be what you call, my blood relative. By your understanding, Gnar, being substantially younger than myself, could be my…'child.'"

"You've got to be kidding me!" I said in awe.

"No, Mi-kal. You see, in our society, at the age equivalent of roughly twenty one of your Earth years, at the so-called prime of our physical purity, we make what you might call 'genetic donations' to our Institution of Population Maintenance."

My mouth dropped open. "You mean sperm banks?" I asked.

"Well, yes, sort of, Mi-kal. You see, all…males make a sperm contribution, and all females make a similar contribution of ovum. These…deposits are immediately assigned lot numbers by parties who are unaware of the donor's identity. At this point, they are closely examined and tested for purity, viability, potential, and overall ability to withstand storage. Those that do not meet the necessary criteria for maintenance are disposed of.

"A small percentage of all remaining lots are separated, mixed with an undisclosed number of other lots, and stored, or frozen, for lack of a better term in your English, for later fertilization purposes."

"Keep going," I said excitedly.

"These mixed lots may be stored for one year or a thousand years. Due to our zero population growth manifests, it is only when a member of our society...'releases', or passes, as you call it, that a new child is conceived. The new child will be of the same gender, and will be given the transcended one's name."

"Wait a minute." I jumped in, "someone before you who died left you his name?"

"Yes," Trr answered, "and there is only one person named Trr, with my spelling, in our society. My name is mine alone, until I pass it on, along with its history, to my descendent."

"But how do you know it's your descendent?" I insisted.

"Because we are all related, and because he will bear my name. In truth, we could be half brothers, but the fact of the matter is that anyone in my society, who is twenty one years younger than myself, may in fact, be my offspring."

"Come on, that's got to be confusing," I insisted. "How can you care about a child that you're not even sure of?"

Trr glared at me with a look that verged on total disdain. I could tell that he was holding back his impulse to get angry. And then, almost immediately, he smiled.

"*Every* child is my child, Mi-kal. And every child is Gnar's and Zwig's, and we treat them that way. With love, understanding, patience, caring, nurturing, concern, and devotion. And the children all respect us as a parent.

"Every adult male is like my brother, and every adult female is like my sister, and we all love and care about one another. We realize that the likelihood of an actual direct blood tie is improbable, but we know positively, that we all share the same diverse ancestry, and we have made sure of it.

"When a child is conceived we are careful to ensure that no incestual, improper, unhealthy, or genetically incompatible match is made. No two of us has the same two parents, and none of us can inadvertently take on a parent or a sibling as a companion."

There was a long pause, while I tried to comprehend it all, but the more I thought about it, the more questions I had.

"Mi-kal, do not overly concern yourself with the specifics of our ways. Only know that it works very well for us. Your world should only know the love and kinship we experience on ours."

"But how are the children raised, and who raises them?" I asked softly.

"Remember the rotations I told you of earlier?" Trr asked. I nodded. "Well, one of those rotations is involved with…child care. Every individual is expected to participate in the basic education of, rearing of, feeding of, and nurturing of the children in our society. Granted, some are better at it than others, but all participate."

"But what if I decided that child-rearing was what I wanted to do with my life?" I interjected.

"Then with the proper continued education, after graduation, and after fulfilling the required number of rotations, as one rotates up the ladder of expertise, one eventually may choose a given occupation as one's primary area of concentration, and rotate, almost exclusively within the parameters of that area of societal concern. If one aspires to a higher level of decision making, planning, or authority, one goes before a committee comprised of one's peers and coworkers and is judged on fitness, according to the preparedness standards set forth and displayed by the practitioner. At any time one wishes to leave one's area of expertise, one can, just by requesting a transfer. This is the reason for completing three educational degrees. In your society, one finds oneself unhappy or disillusioned with one's chosen profession, but finds that one is ill-suited to do anything else. We offer retraining and reeducation at any time, but one must continue to work a minimal amount of hours while studying. Most first professions are chosen between the Earth ages of fifty and seventy five. I pretty much always knew what I wanted to do, Mi-kal."

"And what was that?" I asked.

"Why, this, of course! Trr exclaimed, smiling. Since I was a child, I wanted to travel the cosmos, expand my horizons, escape the banalities of sameness!"

"How did you know for sure?" I questioned.

"I really shouldn't share this with you, Mi-kal, because I do find it marginally embarrassing, but when I was a child of, say, seventeen or eighteen of your Earth years, I was walking beside a throughway, when I spotted a small cruiser with its…motion generators in a holding mode, in other words, someone had left the engine running.

"Now, you must understand, Mi-kal, that we don't own, in your vernacular, transportational devices, or TDs, we merely take temporary possession of them as needed, and drop them off at our destination. So, for all intents and purposes, everyone collectively owns all of these modes of transport, while not individually owning any of them."

It sounded to me like Trr was trying to justify stealing a car, by saying that it was a loaner anyway.

"That's more than likely true," Trr interrupted my train of thought, "but nevertheless, I did, without prior authorization, take possession of said vehicle, and as you might say, 'put the pedal to the metal.'

"I had only intended to take it around the block once or twice, but I couldn't help myself, I aimed that floater towards the stars and took off!"

This was fascinating! Trr was projecting images into my mind as he talked. I could almost see what he saw. It was exhilarating!

"I kicked the anti-gravitational polarization module into maximum repel, and soared off into the heavens...!" Trr paused.

"Yeah?" I said breaking the silence. "What happened next?"

"I got lost," Trr said. " I ended up ripping the bottom out of the vehicle when I crash landed, with no fuel, on a small moon. I was trapped inside with a limited supply of life support.

"I was very lucky that I had been tracked, by what you would call 'the authorities,' who rescued me and returned me for re-orientation.

"I went through that for two years, but it was worth it. I knew what I wanted to do with my life, after that, and I studied twice as hard to achieve my goals. And you know what Mi-kal, they encouraged me to become successful. They taught me everything I needed to know to be successful. They didn't hold me back or discourage me. They helped me channel my energies in a positive direction. They helped me find my niche, and I became an asset to my society, instead of a burden."

"You know, we could use some programs like that here," I remarked.

"Yes, I know, Mi-kal. You need them badly. We don't

have…penal institutions. We have re-orientation institutes."

"Come on, Trr, that can't work on everyone. There have to be a few hard cases."

"You're correct," he said, "and they are subjected to intense behavioral modification techniques, which are physically painless but can be psychologically devastating. Eventually, they all find a place in our society where they do the least amount of harm to anyone, including themselves. Don't get me wrong, they are functional and aware, but must wear behavior modifiers, or BMs as we refer to them, which stimulate the appropriate pain or pleasure centers, according to one's current activities."

"That sounds cruel," I said.

"It isn't," he replied, "they feel completely normal until they begin thinking along dissocial lines. Then they are mentally 'prodded' back into more socially acceptable modes of behavior. If they can exhibit, for an extended period of time, that they no longer have these negative behavioral inclinations, the BMs are removed. All the while, they were never, for any substantial period of time, deprived of their 'freedom.'"

"Well," I said, "given a choice between a BM and prison, I guess I'd take the BM." We both chuckled. It was nice to learn that they weren't all "perfect."

"Today," Trr continued, "theft of a TD is virtually impossible. Now all vehicles are voice- and print-coded at the time of taking possession, rendering it usable only to the party who has legal operational privileges. These codes can only be changed, at the time of surrender of said TD, by the party involved. So you see, Mi-kal, you can no longer exit a vehicle while leaving it on, nor can you enter it unless it is coded out to you. I like to believe that my own little adventure helped bring about these changes."

Was this a little egotistical pride I heard coming from Trr? I wondered.

"Leaving some small degree of positive influence on our society is very important to us, Mi-kal. Everyone wants, directly or indirectly, to leave one's 'mark' on society. If one's actions are negative ones, they are admonished, counseled, and the event is never socially discussed again. It certainly is not glorified, or left lying around as a negative influence on the minds of our children. We would never make a 'movie of the week' out of someone's misfortune. Fame and recognition can only be attained through positive acts. We believe that breeding antisocial behavior, by the glorification of it, is insanity."

"You know a hell of a lot about us 'Earthlings,' don't you?" I said distrustingly.

"That's my job," he replied.

"What else is your 'job'?" I retorted. Trr paused again. "Shall I continue, Mi-kal?"

He obviously wasn't going to tell me any more than he planned, or was authorized to. "You are mistaken, Mi-kal. My associates have expressed serious reservations concerning my exchange of relevant information with you, on your behalf. I, however, have…felt that your better understanding of us, and our culture, could only facilitate familiarity, and perhaps inspire greater trust on your part."

"Yeah sure," I said, "I bet you tell that to all of your hostages."

"You are not a hostage, Mi-kal. You are free to leave whenever you choose!"

Was I? I wasn't too sure. Trr smiled and asked, "Shall we continue?"

"Yes," I nodded.

"Our 'government' has a similar structure to your own. However, we have no need for what you call a president. We have twenty-five or more representatives, depending upon the importance, or weight, of the sociological decision to be made, who sit in the Assembly. These twenty-five individuals rotate the 'chairmanship,' as you would call it, on a daily basis. This way, no one individual is prone to abuse his temporary position because he knows he will be subjected to the same inconsiderations in the days that immediately follow by future chairpersons.

"Four or five of these assemblymen step down each year, according to seniority and are replaced by members of the Subassembly, a membership body of some five hundred or more, who vote on the fitness of those who are eligible for promotion.

"The assemblymen who have stepped down are free to become members of the Subassembly and can be reassigned to the Assembly, but no sooner than the equivalent of ten Earth years, for another five-year term.

"The Subassembly is composed of a few former Assembly members, and by and large contains learned individuals from all of the fields of rotation. Specialists, instructors, and others with important concerns are either voted in by those they represent, or by petition, due to the importance of their concerns, by the Subassembly itself. Just as one rotates out of the Assembly, so does one rotate out of the Subassembly. Eventually, everyone, theoretically, has a chance to participate directly in higher government."

"What do you mean theoretically?" I inquired.

"Mi-kal, many do not choose to serve on the Assembly or in the Subassembly. To require someone to make decisions they do not choose to make concerning others, or to require them to do so when they are unfit, or ill-prepared, would be an infringement on their freedom, and the freedom of all members of society. It would be equally disadvantageous to require everyone to do my job. Many are ill-suited for it, or have no desire to engage in this enterprise."

"I agree," I said, "but suppose I'm a lunatic or something? Do they still have to let me voice my opinion?"

"Yes," Trr answered. "You may voice your opinion, briefly and succinctly. You will be heard, and your position will be considered, if only for a moment or two, before the Subassembly votes and then continues with the next matter. Therefore, there is no one individual to blame, or for you to feel disadvantaged by, but rather a large number of your peers have judged your position as not tenable at that time.

"No one is shown disrespect, and in return, disrespect may not be shown towards the Sub-assembly or the Assembly itself. However, you may be granted an appeal date after ninety days, if you so request.

"You guys seem to have it all together," I said respectfully. "We have a tendency to let a few old narrow-minded individuals make most of our decisions for us and then virtually pick who their successors will be. We call it a free election, but we are told which individuals we have to choose from. If you don't have a great deal of money, or are not backed by people who do, then your name will never surface and your ideas will never be heard.

"There are many professors, and other brilliant individuals in private industry, who are much better suited to influence this country, and to move it forward, then the power-hungry egomaniacs we currently are forced to elect. Unless you sell out, in our system, you don't stand a chance of being elected to higher office. Our leaders practice politricks, not politics. Maybe we should just call them politricians, it would be more fitting."

"Yes, I have observed in detail the...circus you people call the electoral process," Trr added. "We are very disappointed that it has only marginally improved over the past few centuries.

"You have made tremendous progress on a scientific or technological basis, but you continue to rapidly regress on a sociological or ethical basis. You are, if you don't mind my saying it, all but totally inept in the matters that should concern you most.

"Education, crime, standards of social courtesies, such as dress, grooming, male-female relationships, drugs—including your alcohol—pornography, physical and psychological abuse, and trivial matters concerning race and religion are at abhorrent levels.

"We would no more allow a group of you into our society then we would knowingly introduce a plague. You...people are pathetic at best, and totally disgusting at your worst. You are, in many ways, worse than the animals you are surrounded by. No animal subjects itself willingly to the levels of degradation in which most of you wallow, with your petty competitiveness, greed, lust, lying, selfishness, materialistic backstabbing, insincerity, and overt callousness towards one another. You have allowed your so-called freedom to enslave you. I don't know how any of you keep your sanity! I'm not sure any of you have. Your society, no, your world, is insane, and at times I question my own sanity for choosing to observe this morass of iniquity.

"It sickens me to see your divine potential denigrated to its lowest common denominators. You people let the worst in you prevail. You are the embarrassment of your galaxy and a scourge to the cosmos!"

I had tears in my eyes. Whether they were tears of anger or tears of revelation, I'm not sure. I fought back the lump in my throat and tried to speak. Trr turned to me with tears in his own eyes and said, "Mi-kal, I don't want to hear it. Good night!"

And the world went black.

Chapter Six
I Am Nothing

I woke up in a dream. Whether it was one of *my* dreams or one of theirs, I'm not sure. By now I was almost totally disoriented, no longer able to make the subtle distinctions concerning fact and fiction, reality and fantasy, truth and falsehood, or consciousness and dreaming that we all make on a day-to-day basis

I could no longer determine which thoughts were mine, and which were theirs. All I knew was that I was back in junior high school. In front of me stood this weird kid that no one really liked. He kept insisting he was from another planet, and nothing we asked him or called him would make him deviate from his story. In my dream, his name was Edgar Simpson Percival. I'm pretty sure it wasn't his real name, but it was in my dream.

Edgar wore thick glasses with brown turtle-shell frames. They were held in place by an elastic eyeglass band, probably because they were otherwise too heavy to stay up on his narrow face.

When you looked Edgar in the eye, his face appeared distorted through the large "coke-bottle" lenses. His forehead and skull seemed inordinately large, compared to his face and body.

Edgar dressed strangely also. It wasn't that his clothing was all that different, it was just different than what the "cool kids" wore to school. Plaid shirts and striped pants weren't in.

He always had a large pile of books under his arm. In junior high this was exceedingly strange, because most of his books had nothing to do with any of our classes. The cool kids had backpacks, but not Edgar the nerd, or "dork," as we called him.

I guess I can admit it now, although I wouldn't have then, but I kind of liked Edgar Simpson Percival. He was kind of interesting, like watching a praying mantis is interesting, or maybe a grasshopper. I'm sure you get the idea.

I'm not really sure that Edgar ever really attended our school. He was never in any of my classes, or anyone else's that I knew, for that matter. But he was always standing around before school or at break time, surrounded by students who would constantly ask him insulting or trick questions, which he seemed always to have an answer for.

One day, Edgar disappeared. In the middle of the semester, he just stopped showing up. I never saw him again, until I saw him in my dream.

There he was, in all his glory, only this time we were standing there alone, just the two of us. We seemed to be talking, but I couldn't make out the words at first. In my dream, Edgar and I were friends, not acquaintances, but "I'll come-over-after-school" kind of friends.

We talked about all sorts of unusual things. Edgar knew he was strange, but he couldn't explain why, except to say that he felt like he was "displaced." He felt like he didn't belong on this planet. He felt like he was visiting, or at camp, waiting to be picked up by his parents.

In my dream, Edgar had special powers. He knew when phones were about to ring. He could predict baseball scores days in advance. He could even come up with the names and addresses of some of the cuter girls at school, girls I didn't even think he knew. This was one strange kid, and I was his only friend. What does that say about me?

Anyway, one evening I thought I'd drop by Edgar's house, unannounced, and see what he was up to. There was no car in the driveway, but there was a light coming from Edgar's room, on the side of the house. I thought I'd sneak up and scare him through the window. But when I peeked in, I could hardly see him in the candlelit room.

As I listened, he seemed to be chanting. It sounded like something out of some old movie I'd seen once about witches. While he chanted, he seemed to be focusing on an ashtray, which was sitting just in front of his crossed legs, on the floor. His hands were moving in a repetitive upward motion, as if he was trying to make the ashtray rise. And you know what, it did. I swear it did. It floated about a foot and a half above the floor, about chest high to Edgar, as he sat there.

I couldn't believe it! In fact, I think that's what I said, without intending to say it out loud. "I don't believe it!"

At that instant, Edgar jerked his head to the right, looking towards the window. The ashtray fell and shattered on the floor. I freaked out! I turned and sprinted into the darkness of the night, swearing never to return. No one was going to believe this! And no one did.

Although I'm sure that Edgar never saw me that night, our friendship had ended. He just seemed to know it was me and that

I was a little afraid of him. Edgar hadn't really changed, I had. He seemed weirder than ever after that night. All the other kids called him a freak. I'm not sure why. They hadn't seen what I saw. I guess we just don't take well to those who are a little different from us. Anyway, if I wanted to keep any of my other friends, I knew I had to stop being friends with Edgar. I think he sensed this, and I think it really hurt his feelings.

In my dream, I saw Edgar again, but we were in our late teens by then. I barely recognized him as I was passing by with a couple of my teenage buddies. We stopped. Edgar was dressed up kind of like a magician, wearing white face, like a mime, and he was drawing a small crowd of people. He never spoke, he just performed one inexplicable magic trick after another, to the amazement of the crowd, who kept tossing money into an extra magician's hat, turned upside down on the ground.

I wanted to say something to Edgar, but he stopped me with a glance. He smiled, nodded, bowed, retrieved his extra hat and props, and disappeared around the corner. I tried to catch up with him. As I trotted around the corner, I thought I saw him heading into an alley. I caught up with him and tapped him lightly on the shoulder. He turned around, and I stood face to face with…Trr? The world went black. And then…

Was I awake? Was I asleep? Was I anything at all?

There I was, staring out into nothing. No sound, no wind, no color, no nothing. And that was exactly how I felt, I was nothing. I was no one. I had no name, no body, no…nothing. I would have closed my eyes, but I had no eyelids. I had no nothing.

Descartes was wrong. I'm thinking, but I am not. I am nothing, and nothing is me. Now I know how God must have felt, before he created everything. Alone. Completely alone. Alone without a clue. Where do I start? What do I use to create this universe when there is nothing to make it out of? There is nothing. I haven't made anything yet. I need something to fling, something to breathe life into, but how do I make something, how do I make anything out of nothing?

And if I find something, where did it come from? Was it here before me? Of course not. If it was, then someone or something else must have created it. Perhaps my mother. Everything has a mother. All life comes from other life, except the first life. Is that me? Am I truly alone? Am I truly all that there is? And if so, where did I come from?

I don't remember having these thoughts yesterday. But then, when was yesterday? How did the concept even come to me, because there are no days, no nights, no sun, no moon, no stars, no…nothing. It's easy being everything and everywhere when you are nothing and nowhere. I am lost. I am abandoned, and there is no hope for creation, save that which is a figment of my imagination.

If I am to create a world out of nothingness, then can it exist except in the tenuous consciousness of my blank mind? Blank, because I have never seen, touched, tasted, smelled, or heard anything, ever, anywhere at anytime. I am *la tabula rasa,* the blank slate. Ah, but a blank slate is still a slate nonetheless, and I, I am…nothing.

Where do I begin? Do I start now, or should I wait a millennium or two? Should I have begun a millennium ago? Does it matter? Does time even exist? Have I even created time yet? If not, then how shall I mark it? How can I decide to begin now, when I don't know when now is? How can I know anything, when I have experienced nothing, and only nothing?

To formulate a concept, I must base that concept on something. To make a change in the structure of a thing, that thing must first exist, but how can it exist until I create it? And out of what shall I first create it so that I can change it?

Change seems impossible without existence, and nothing exists to change, because I haven't yet created anything, and I haven't yet created anything because I don't know how, and I don't know how because I've never created anything before now, and there is no now because there is no time, and there is no time because I have no point of reference.

I am lost. I am alone. I am nothing.

Surely this is how God must have felt.

What is that? There was something that flitted across my mind. There it is again! A story. I'm not sure where it came from, but...Listen.

Many years in the future, a baby was born. By then, science had advanced to a near miraculous state, and medical science was able to achieve virtually any task set before it, save actual resurrection of the dead. But they had achieved the next best thing. Heart, head, arm, leg, genitals, and countless other transplants were commonplace, but this baby had suffered such devastating physical deformity, due to the severity of the accident its mother had succumbed to, that nothing short of removing the brain to save the baby's life was even plausible.

Upon very close examination, the baby's brain was diagnosed as having the potential of true genius. The diagnostic equipment was reading off the scale, and many specialists were called in for consultation.

There could only be one conclusion, the baby's brain must be saved for humanity's sake. Although there was no problem preserving the brain, or even providing it with an artificial body, the problem stemmed from the fact that, as an artificial life form, it would be impossible for the baby to lead a normal life. In other words, the baby's genius would not be beneficial to mankind if the baby had no real life experiences to draw from. To help mankind, the baby must first understand what it means to a person, with wants and needs, likes and dislikes, by experiencing pain and pleasure. It was agreed that a controlled environment would best enhance the baby's potential.

Oh, yes, there was one other minor problem. In the future, the world had become a little too sterile. Human beings had somehow lost much of their humanity. They had forgotten what it was like to care truly about one another, to fear the unknown, and to stare in wonder at the world around them. Everything, for the most part, was taken for granted, and those things that were once cherished, were all but forgotten. Things like family, friendship, love, hate, admiration, envy, triumph and failure. Humanity had all but lost that which distinguished it from the machines.

If the baby were to help society, then it was important that the baby be "raised" in a world that no longer existed. A world more like today.

The decision was made to place the baby's brain inside one of their most sophisticated computers. They connected all of the necessary life support. They named the brain Pat, and loaded the pertinent data into the computer banks to create a world long since past. One with trees, animals, clouds, automobiles, and families. They said a primitive silent prayer, handed down from old wives' tales, and pushed the button.

Pat's world came alive with a blur of sensations. Light, heat, cold, pain, shock, and a flood of tears asking *Why?* The gentle arms that enfolded Pat were answer enough. Pat was, for all intents and purposes, alive and kicking.

The scientists programmed Pat's mother to give Pat a new name and identity. On a daily, nay, hourly basis, new data was fed into Pat's world. They programmed Pat to crawl, eventually to walk, and even to stumble and fall. Skinned knees and elbows were not unheard of for Pat, nor were spills, childhood diseases, colds, wet diapers, and the like.

Due to the fact that Pat's world was a product of Pat's mind, and not subject to "real time," the scientists were able to speed up the maturation process by speeding up the influx of data. Pat was not aware of this, because Pat had no other reference points, save those in Pat's world.

Pat was growing up normal in a normal world of childhood friends and classmates. Crushes on teachers gave way to puppy love, and eventually to adult love.

Pat was as normal as Pat could be. Life was not all sweetness and light, nor was it always A's on report cards. There were minor triumphs as well as disappointments.

One day, the scientists decided to test Pat. They wanted to see if Pat had any idea that Pat wasn't normal. They wanted to know how Pat would react to finding out that Pat was Pat, and not who Pat thought Pat was.

They agreed that a subtle approach would best serve their purpose. If Pat reacted with certainty and acceptance of this new-found identity, then they felt Pat would be ready for the next step, reintegration into their world, the world of the future, leaving behind the illusory world Pat knew.

If Pat rejected this disclosure, however, it was decided to permit Pat to continue in the present mode, until some future point in time when they deemed Pat to be better prepared to accept the truth.

But how would they tell Pat, that Pat was Pat?

They decided to write a book. In this book they would introduce Pat to a few strange new ideas and concepts. And when Pat was somewhat off guard, they broke the news.

YOU ARE PAT.

Yes, you. The one who is reading or hearing these words, right this instant, is Pat. We're not kidding. You really are Pat. You, the one sitting there.

You. You are Pat. You are not the person you think you are. You are the person we made you to be.

If you can read or hear this, you are Pat. The world around you is an illusion of our creation.

Do you believe that you are Pat? Remember, you can't lie to us, we are monitoring your responses, right this instant.

If you do not believe that you are Pat, prove that you are not.

You can't prove it because you *are* Pat.

You only think you are where you are now, but you are not. Everything and everyone around you, is a product of your imagination. They don't really exist. Only you exist, not your world. We created your world for you. You are Pat.

If you believe you are Pat, stop now.

Very well, then. Continue...

Hi, Pat. This is a good place to stop if you're religious. Please do not hold me responsible for any further disruption of your belief system.

Some people are not ready for enlightenment. Some are not prepared to have their world shaken. It is not my desire to cause harm to anyone through revealing antitruths. If your mind is open, then the way you see life will change. For some, this change will be very subtle, for others, severe.

Some will begin to question many of their most heartfelt beliefs. For some, I fear, this may not be to their immediate advantage.

The plausibility of what I am about to tell you is high. Higher, perhaps, than what you currently believe. I ask only that if you continue, you do not hold me personally accountable hereafter.

I mean you no harm. Please do not wish harm to come to me.

Read this with love and understanding, not as a personal insult. Please don't kill the messenger.

Chapter Seven

The Keeper of the Globe

I woke up in my own bed. I believed it was my own bed. At least I believed I was awake. I couldn't be sure of anything anymore.

I pride myself in saying that I have never been high or drunk on anything in my entire life, but I'm sure that this was in some ways, far worse.

I was confused. All of the who, what, when, where, why, and hows were lost to me. All I was absolutely certain of was that I couldn't be certain of anything. The dreams had somehow stolen my confidence. I had succumbed to doubt and was being held prisoner by my own mind. I needed help.

I'm not sure what a nervous breakdown is. I'm not sure I was having one. I don't believe I did, but who knows? I could be wrong. Oh yeah, there was one more thing I was sure of. I wanted the dreams to end. I just wanted my old stable, boring life back. I'd had enough lunacy to last me a lifetime. And so, I decided to make a supreme effort to get control of myself, to get my life back on the right track; to forget these dreams, and get on with living.

Apparently, my mind had other ideas. Two or three days later,

I found myself back in the company of these familiar strangers. I don't know how I got there. I didn't drive anywhere in my dream, I was just there.

Overall, I felt pretty good. I was rested, and I wasn't feeling any particular animosity or anxiety connected with this, our latest encounter.

All three of them greeted me telepathically. I politely responded in thought. They nodded, I nodded. They smiled, I smiled. I guess we all felt a little awkward.

In retrospect, I guess they were feeling a little guilty for what they were doing to me. Of course, it wasn't enough to make them stop, and, of course, I may be a bit presumptuous in assuming that they are even capable of feeling guilt. In fact, by this time, I wasn't sure they were capable of feeling anything the way we humans feel things.

"Of course we do, Mi-kal." Trr interrupted my train of thought. "I admit that our emotions tend to be…experienced at a less intense level than your own, due to our training, but we still retain the full spectrum of feelings."

"Feelings like what?" I asked. "Like pity or superiority?"

"Yes," Trr responded," but also emotions such as joy, kinship, annoyance, and anxiety."

"What about love and hate?" I asked sternly.

Trr seemed to hang his head slightly. "Mi-kal, I wish to apologize for some of the things I said to you upon our last meeting. I do fully understand that I should not have caused you to feel directly responsible for the antisocial behavior of your entire species. It's not your fault."

"Damn, man," I interjected, "I know it's not my fault! Where do you people get off criticizing us? At least we are capable of honest emotions, without your phony justifications and rationalizations of every single little twinge of feeling. I'm glad I can feel things. I'm glad I feel compassion for others. I' m glad I still have the capacity to feel *real* feelings and not some artificially contrived 'proper response to a given experience.' At least we still have each other. At least we have mothers and fathers whom we love and who love us. To be honest with you, Trr, I think you're jealous of us. I think you freaks have lost the capacity to love. I wouldn't give up one day as a real human being for a hundred years of this living death you call life! You may screw my head up about a lot of things, you may have me so turned around that I don't know if or when I'm coming or going, but damn it, I still have my humanity. I still know that I love my world, and the people in it, even if it is some damned illusion! And guess what, you can't take that away from me, oh no, you'll *never* take that away from me!"

Trr had tears in his eyes. Real tears. Tears like we cry. And for the first time, he stepped forward, and embraced me. Then, in a soft voice, almost a whisper, he said, "I know, Mi-kal, and it is that love that gives us hope for you. As long as your people don't lose the love, the basic empathy and caring for one another, you'll make it.

"Your capacity to love one another is the only reason we are still here. It's the only reason we are personally concerned about the direction in which your world is precariously heading. As long as you love one another, we'll be here, watching and waiting to welcome you into the brotherhood of the stars."

I was stunned. Trr really seemed to be sincere. For the first time, I didn't feel like he was manipulating me. For the first time I felt he was actually my friend.

I looked over at Zwig and Gnar. They were crying too. They quickly turned and scurried off to their respective places in front of their monitoring screens.

"You people really do understand us, don't you?" I asked Trr.

"Yes, Mi-kal, better than you think. We're really not that different from each other. Under this 'second skin,' we are still capable of bleeding. We cry, we love, and we long for home and miss our friends."

"Well," I said, "with God's help, I'm sure you'll see your home and friends again. Do you have a wife, or what did you call them, a companion?"

"Not anymore," he answered.

"But don't you get…horny, or something?" I whispered, embarrassed.

"Mi-kal, I am almost one thousand years old. I left those desires hundreds of years behind me, with the rest of my hair, my original teeth, and a few dozen original organs."

"But don't you miss it all? I insisted.

"Not in the traditional sense," he answered, "besides, that's one of the functions of the dream machine. We can relive or re-experience those pleasant memories whenever we choose. Remember, Mi-kal, sex is only partly physical. All of the best parts happen in your head. Real love, real ecstasy, and real fulfillment, are functions of the mind, not the body.

"If your mind isn't participating in the sexual act, then no amount of physical stimulation will bring you satisfaction. Conversely, we have found that we can achieve far greater levels of ecstasy, through thought transfer, then we could otherwise. I can do things to you with my mind, that I could never do with my body."

I was blushing now. "Hey," I said jokingly, "don't get too close!" Trr laughed.

"Don't worry, Mi-kal, it is forbidden."

"Yeah, God doesn't like us to mix up the species too much!" I added.

"It's not that, Mi-kal. Before we took this assignment, we took a vow of non-interference."

"What!" I exclaimed. "Then what do you call what you've been doing to me?"

"Witnessing," he answered bluntly. What we have done to and with you will have no lasting effect."

"It will on me!" I exclaimed. Trr didn't respond. Instead, he changed the subject.

"Mi-kal, your people have an intriguing preoccupation with religious practices."

"Yeah, so what?" I asked defensively.

"Well, it's just that we have traveled all over the universe, and we have yet to find this God you seem so obsessed with. Why do you continue to cling to such antiquated belief systems now that your technology is clearly showing you that there is no one out there?"

"You were out there," I responded, "and we didn't even believe you existed. So obviously, we are willing to admit that we don't know everything, unlike you."

"By the way, Trr, what *do* you people believe in anyway?"

"We believe in ourselves, Mi-kal, and we believe in each other. Most of us have long since abandoned our ancestor's superstitions and fairy tales."

"Then who tells you what's right and wrong? Whose law do you live by, just the ones you made up, with your Assemblies and Subassemblies and rotations, and all that other garbage?"

"It isn't garbage, Mi-kal. We believe that each of us has the capacity to differentiate between right and wrong. We hold ourselves accountable for all of our own actions. We don't blame it on some...devil, or evil entity.

"Negative things happen. That is an irrefutable law of nature. But it is also relative. What I may deem to be a negative occurrence may be deemed a positive one by someone else. Gods and devils have nothing to do with it, and if they did exist, they would also have their own good days and bad days.

"We believe that at any given moment, and under any given set of circumstances, we should act in such a manner that it would be appropriate for anyone and everyone to act in the same manner, in the same situation, for the same reasons. In other words, on the surface, it would appear to be a wrongful act for me to strike you. However, if my reasons for striking you are admirable, for instance, to save your life or to defend my own, then I can readily say that under the same set of circumstances, and for the same reasons, it would be appropriate for you to strike me. Breaking the basic rules of conduct is admissible, given the circumstances.

"Let me give you another example. In your culture, it is deemed sinful to engage in an act of sexual intercourse with another adult if you are married to a third party. However, it would, in my culture, and I assume in your own, be far more sinful or inappropriate to refuse to engage in said intercourse if your very life, or the life of your spouse or children, were contingent upon it. In such a case, committing adultery would be the heroic or appropriate thing to do."

"It sounds to me like you're saying that the end justifies the means," I said.

"Not at all, Mi-kal. I am saying that the circumstances demand a proper response, and that sometimes that response may be, under different circumstances, a wrongful act, or sin as you call it. The same applies to acts of lying, stealing, and other sins.

"The most important factor involved in any decision to do or not to do something is to ask oneself, what if everyone did the same thing I am doing? Would they be justified, under the same circumstances? And suppose they were doing it to you. Would you understand why, and would you forgive them?"

"I see what you mean. It's kind of like our 'do unto others' credo. Does it also apply to killing someone?" I inquired.

"Yes, even that," he said. "If I take a life, without adequate provocation, then I forfeit my own."

"Does that include abortion?" I asked.

Trr hesitated. "No, that is different," he responded. "We define life as the ability to think and act of your own accord. A first trimester...fetus, as you call it, has not yet developed a brain capable of cognitive skills. The fetus, early on, has not developed arms, legs, or many other appendages or organs. A fetus is not yet a person, it is a 'potential person', and potential persons are not afforded the same rights to life as a person who has developed into a cognitive being. After all, every ovum a woman carries, and every sperm a man produces, is a potential person. Each one is different, and if permitted, would become an actualized person. It would be insanity to attempt to actualize all potential persons merely because they are deemed to be human life. Every living cell in a human's genetic makeup, through cloning, has the potential of becoming a new person. Does this mean you should be held responsible for every cell of your body? Of course not. We realize the difference between cells and fertilized eggs, but the difference is only by degree.

"A fetus in the first trimester is absolutely incapable of survival outside of the mother's womb. This does not suggest, however, that the potential person will not quickly develop into an actualized person, sometime during the second trimester. This is why we would not perform an abortion, except to save the mother's life, after the first trimester."

"Do you people perform abortions?" I asked.

"Virtually never, because intercourse is forbidden before the genetic donation is completed and sterilization through medical means is achieved. Our abortions are performed by ingesting a tablet, which terminates the pregnancy by inducing premature labor. This tablet can only be administered and taken under the direct supervision of a specialist. Afterwards, both female and male undergo counseling."

"But how do you keep them from doing it again?" I asked.

"Mi-kal, how do you keep anyone from killing, stealing, lying, or from engaging in any form of antisocial or self-destructive behavior? Proper education and strict adherence to societal rules are insisted upon. Once one clearly understands that a certain behavior is unacceptable, or wrong, as you would put it, and the many reasons why it is wrong, including the far-reaching implications of such behavior, a rational, well-educated, and properly counseled individual will desist in such behavior.

"We have virtually no physical altercations, theft, drug abuse, teenage pregnancy, social diseases, or the accompanying mental disorders they propagate. Ultimately, Mi-kal, any and all disagreements are settled by one party prevailing over the other in a civil manner. In your society, 'might makes right' has been the order of the day. In ours, that which is true and just must prevail.

"We are mature enough to agree to disagree on most matters. Because we personally own so little, and yet collectively have so much, we have all but eliminated disputes over property, fidelity, and ethics. Fairness makes right, and rational people can always come to a reasonable and fair solution to any dispute. There is never a need to 'bully' one's way into an advantageous position over others."

"When you say you have few possessions, how does that work? Suppose I needed a new VCR, but I didn't have the money to purchase one?" I inquired.

"Then you would merely take your old VCR to an exchange facility, where you would receive a new one, with all of the latest innovations, if you so desired. The old one would be disassembled and…recycled," Trr answered.

"How can you afford to do that?" I asked incredulously.

"Simple, Mi-kal," he replied. "If everyone works, then everyone is entitled to the same advantages. There are no class distinctions. No job provides greater physical wealth than another; however, greed and hoarding are discouraged. Why would I want to take something in your possession if I can have my own by merely requesting one? And furthermore, why would I not share my possessions with you, when I can always obtain more? Prestige is not earned by what one possesses, but by what personal level of achievement one has attained."

"But don't you ever run out of stuff?" I questioned. "I mean, suppose they're all out of VCRs?"

"Then one will be forthcoming soon. However, Mi-kal, this almost never happens because we closely monitor supply and demand trends. We anticipate shortages and produce a small surplus of that commodity. If additional commodities are needed, in a specific area, say a certain artificial organ is in short supply, then additional workers are brought in from another similar facility, within the same area of rotation, whose own supply levels may be more than adequate, and on a temporary basis, they are employed in the production of said replacement organ. Balance is the key to all things, Mi-kal. Never too much of one thing or too little of another. Balance."

"Well, it sounds too good to be true to me," I stated flatly. "Why would I want to work hard, if I can't get over?" I asked.

"*Everyone* has 'gotten over,' Mi-kal. Can't you see that? We have supervisors, not bosses, and everyone supervises the supervisor. We have enough integrity to want to do a good job and to improve our performance, our facility, and ultimately, our society. We take great pride in our achievements, whether they are personal ones or the achievements of our society and our world as a whole.

"With our technology, we have all but eliminated strenuous labor. Most of our skills are technical ones, and great effort is taken, on an ongoing basis, to keep them from becoming too…'boring,' as you would say.

"At the end of each rotation, excellence in each field is recognized and acknowledged. Usually a small award is issued to commemorate one's achievement. We don't feel jealous of another's accomplishments, because their work in no way prevents us from achieving excellence as well.

"It isn't a race, it's more like surpassing a standard of normalcy. Anyone can do it if they set their mind to it, and no one can hinder you from your achievements, save yourself.

"Later, however, when the time comes to vote someone into representing us in the Sub-assembly, we do so based on their achievements and their efforts."

"What about God?" I asked. "I know you don't believe in one, but how can you be so sure? A lot of people here on Earth work hard, or try to do the right thing, like helping others, because they wish to please God."

"Mi-kal, before the Resurrection, over a million years ago, many of our ancestors believed in a god. Not your god, but a god nonetheless. They called him 'The Keeper.' 'The Keeper of the Globe.'

"Unlike your God, the Keeper was seen as a kind of 'divine scientist.' It was believed that this heavenly scientist, while working in His laboratory, decided to create our universe inside a large crystalline globe. With the aid of others, He added all of the necessary components to create spheres, such as planets, stars, and all of the various matter and anti-matter elements needed to achieve the proper balance.

"He stirred the concoction, pulling all of the substantive matter towards the center of the globe, and then He added the spice, the spice of life. 'Ah, it is beautiful,' He must have thought, as He observed His universe through various instruments of magnification. Perhaps it needed a little bit more of this, or a little bit more of that! Perhaps it needed to be left alone and studied with careful scrutiny. After all, if the Keeper was displeased with his creation, he could always destroy it and start again.

"And he might have done just that, if he hadn't noticed something peculiar, something exceptional, nay, something divine!"

I could see Trr's pictures, whirling through my mind.

"The Keeper called to the others, who, looking through His instruments, saw what He had seen: tiny, almost infinitesimally small organisms, beginning to thrive on a few of the larger clumps of matter that were slowly swirling in the center of the globe. Mind you, what must have been but a moment to the Keeper was in all likelihood a generation to the organisms, but it must have been nothing less than remarkable to observe.

"My ancestors believed that this is how our universe came into being, through divine creation, and that they were being watched by the Keeper, who either approved or disapproved of their behavior. Many believed that if their behavior offended the Keeper, He would be driven to destroy their world. He would simply pluck it out of the universe, and smash it between His thumb and forefinger.

"It would amount to no great loss to Him but would obviously be catastrophic to their world.

"Every effort was made on the part of some factions to placate the Keeper by acknowledging His presence. Not that they could see Him, or had any proof of His existence, save their own existence as evidence.

"Temples were constructed to glorify Him. People gathered together and attempted to communicate with the Keeper through collective thought transfer. They humbled themselves before Him, and begged Him for understanding and guidance. After all, pleasing the Keeper was the only assurance they had against destruction.

"Many wore tributes or totems as constant reminders that their behavior was being observed. Others shunned the Believers, and opted for differing points of view. Some sects believed that they were too small for the Keeper to see, just as He was too large for them to see. And at any rate, with the time differential, due to the quantum displacement of relative time, they believed that they would be born, age, and die, before the Keeper would have time to 'fish them out.' These so-called Heretics, along with those who flatly believed that the Keeper never existed, and those who believed He had either long since lost interest, or had Himself, as you would say, passed away, began to formulate new theories about the nature of the universe. Oh, you would not believe the wars that broke out over this issue alone! Or maybe you would. At any rate, Mi-kal, the Believers felt that total destruction was imminent if they could not bring the Heretics back into the faith. They were positive that the Keeper thrived on subservience and obvious displays of adulation.

"They had their equivalent of the Christian soldier, who marched across continents, converting or destroying other cultures that would not or could not conform, due to their own sacred beliefs. This war, in different manifestations, would grow and subside for thousands upon thousands of years. Millions of people died so that the Way of the Keeper might prevail. To Hell with what the Keeper *really* wanted, the only thing that mattered was that they acted in His name.

"Those who believed in Him crushed the will of the heathens who did not. Those who did not believe tried systematically to exterminate factions of those who did. All for the sake of the

Keeper of the Globe, who at the very most, may have been mildly amused by the insignificance of it all.

"Mi-kal, why would you care if two tribes of ants were fighting over their belief in you? Ants are powerless to be of any real significance to your world. They can only effectively shape their own world, and you can only watch them, or not, or destroy them or not, but the time or compassion you would expend on them would be minimal at best. Only ants truly care about what happens to ants. We don't, not really.

"At any rate, these factions never did come to a true agreement about the Keeper. Even though the wars would subside, each side continued to try to 'influence' the other into submission. They disliked each other, because it was the expected and accepted thing to do. The Believers threatened the Heretics with the 'Holy Wrath of the Keeper,' though he apparently did nothing, although some have sworn they heard Him weeping, while others claimed that He was probably laughing.

"A time came when the "Technologists" had come to power. It was their turn to exert their influence and to voice their point of view on the matter.

"The decision was made to prove or disprove the existence of the Globe through scientific means. That is, the globe that held their universe. Many agreed. Some said it could never be done. Some said they didn't care what the results were, they would not change their beliefs. I fear they would not have changed them even if the Keeper Himself had asked them to. Their minds were stubbornly locked on their own respective 'truths.' Even to consider modifying or abandoning them to an anti-truth, no matter how much enlightenment it brought with it, was out of the question.

"The Technologists used their most advanced equipment to estimate the age, scope, and relative size of the Globe.

"At first, they developed thought enhancers and, later, thought-imaging telescopes in an attempt to 'see' out into the cosmos with their collective minds, to no avail. Next, they developed star-driven probes that were dispersed in all directions and closely monitored, until they individually 'blinked' out of existence.

"Believers claimed that the Keeper had 'confiscated' them all because He disliked their attempts to 'spy' on Him. Other factions claimed the probes had left the outskirts of the galaxies and had smashed themselves against the 'Globe-wall' itself. Still others believed that the probes were still traveling, and that the size of the Globe, like the galaxies, was constantly expanding. At any rate, it didn't work.

"The next attempt was made by sending…something similar to what you might call ionically charged sound waves out into the heavens. They traveled at a considerably greater velocity than the old-fashioned probes.

"The immediate results were spectacular! 'Echoes' were heard, albeit years apart, from all over the universe. From this data, the size of the universe was determined, and our relative location within it was revealed.

"The Believers rejoiced! Great festivals began, with different factions celebrating in the streets. Many Heretics were won over, and they joined the ranks of the Believers. The skeptics were mocked and chastised. Prayer broke out on every corner, and temples were lit anew all over the sphere! And then came the bad news.

"Some of the echoes were not coming back at the prescribed

angle of reflection. In other words, scientists agreed that, if in fact the echoes were echoing off of the sides of the Globe and the Globe did approximate the size and scope they had previously determined, the echoes, or rebounds, should have met a different set of statistical data. Something had gone very wrong.

"According to the new data, the so-called 'Globe,' was anything but round. Instead it took on an ugly, warped, grotesque appearance, somewhat like the shape of a raisin or prune.

"Well, the Believers weren't going to stand for that! The Keeper would never design such an ugly universe! Obviously, the scientists had failed, and the experiment should be repeated with finer calculations and more precise accuracy. After all, this new model was a mockery of the Keeper, and this could not be accepted as the truth!

"The Technologists set about their task anew. It was discovered that their previous transmissions were inadvertently allowed to intercept distant spheres. Galactic fluctuations and black holes also contributed to the distorted data. All of the previously gathered information was useless except as a guide in redirecting their next attempt at measuring the Globe.

"Careful painstaking analysis of the known, or theoretical universe, was stored in massive computer banks. Tremendous amounts of resources, labor, and theoretical knowledge were utilized for over a century to 'fine tune' this new effort and to ensure accuracy.

"Finally, the Technologists were convinced that they had 'ironed out the bugs' in the experiment and were ready to try again. This time, however, they had the full support of the Believers, whose numbers had greatly multiplied. They were now representative of at least a third of the world's population. Success could only ensure their long-awaited triumph over the Heretic factions. Conversions were sure to occur on a rapid and ongoing basis once the new data was collected. Oh, but the Keeper would be proud of their efforts to 'know' Him better and to revel in His handiwork. They were going to paint a technological picture of the Keeper's greatest creation! He would be so pleased."

"Perhaps," I murmured.

"Fully one quarter of their world's wealth and resources had been used to accomplish...nothing. The precisely aimed beams were sent out all over the universe, but only two or three ever echoed back. These were later written off as flukes. The vast majority of the beams never returned, though they waited with bated breath, for a full century, and then another, for any sign, any clue, any return on their investment of time and effort, much of which was at the expense of their respective societies.

"Many of them had sacrificed great wealth, food, and time. The education of their children had suffered. The condition and maintenance of their living and working structures had deteriorated to a state of collapse due to poor preparation and the preoccupation with 'holy revelations' and concerns, rather than life-sustaining ones.

"Factions everywhere became increasingly agitated when they could not seem to rebuild quickly enough, or climb back out of the spiritual and economical slump they were in. The different factions began to prey upon one another. The weaker ones fell quickly, almost willingly, to the larger or more powerful ones.

"In the end, there were only four or five major factions, which dominated their respective hemispheres. All of the joint cooperation and supreme effort they had once displayed towards one great common goal was all but completely forgotten. A once-united world had again become fractioned and intolerant. Power became the rule of the day, and conquest through force or alliance became their 'way.'

"Then it happened. It is still debated to this day which faction was first to initiate the final aggression. Some claim it was one Superfaction, some say another. Regardless, the majority of us believe it was set off by a small, virtually powerless subfaction that had allied itself with a Superfaction and was attempting to solve a now-forgotten minor dispute of some kind with another subfaction on an opposing side by using a single well-aimed nuclear device.

"The explosion devastated virtually all of the targeted subfaction, along with some of their passive, non-militaristic neighbors. Reprisals were insisted upon. Weapon systems were placed on alert, and the guilty parties were threatened to submit to what would have amounted to their total dissolution or be dealt with in the harshest manner. They refused, and they were destroyed.

"The radiation levels were tremendous. Factions all over the sphere felt the aftermath in the form of radiation contamination. Livestock quickly began to die out, and water sources showed unacceptable levels of radiation defilement.

"All factions prepared themselves for the worst, and the worst came. As resources waned, desperate attempts were made by the allied Superfactions to confiscate the basic necessities from their smaller subfactions. Terrorism broke out everywhere, and leaders were assassinated in their sleep. Females and their children, the aged, the weak, even the sick were pushed aside in an 'every man for himself' rush toward survival.

"It was at this time that the exodus began. Each faction loaded its 'chosen' onto spacecrafts and aimed them at the nearest habitable planet, light years away. Nuclear explosions mushroomed in every hemisphere, systematically wiping away faction after faction in their wake. This was the world our ancestors abandoned as they headed for the stars.

"Many did not survive the journey. Many wished they hadn't.

"It was almost inconceivable that the fighting would start anew, almost immediately upon landing on the new planet. We had brought our worst prejudices and factional biases with us. Once again, we set out to destroy ourselves.

"Salvation came in the guise of children. Legend has it that troops from two opposing factions approached each other from opposite sides of a clearing. Taking cover, they trained their weapons upon each other, ready to kill at the first sign of advantage. It was then that they heard the children's laughter. The laughter of innocence that they had all but forgotten in the difficult war-filled years they had lived since arriving on the planet.

"Both factions maneuvered themselves, while retaining their cover, to get a better view of the children. Over towards one end of the clearing were several children playing with a ball. They were excited, screaming with delight, oblivious to the impending danger.

"Men on both sides of the clearing recognized one or more of their own offspring and, in a fit of panic, ran out into the clearing to rescue them from harm, not taking their own safety into consideration. Weapons from both sides were pointed at these two men, ready to strike them down when a clear shot could be made.

"Just as the two men, with contempt in their eyes and hatred in their hearts, snatched up two children apiece, one under each arm, a voice rang out. 'Let them play. Let the children play!' The men froze. Out of the brush stepped an elderly female with radiation scars covering her face and arms. 'They're not hurting anyone. Go ahead and kill each other, if you must, but please, let the children play. They don't understand. They don't know why they should hate one another, so just leave them alone. Let them finish their game. If you love them, let them play.'"

Trr was crying.

"The two men released the children, who gleefully rejoined their friends in the game. They kicked the ball down to the other end of the clearing, leaving the two men fully exposed, in the clear sights of the opposing factions on either side. Everyone held their breath. The two men looked each other in the eye, still unsure as to what to do next.

"One of the men, it makes no difference which, took a deep breath, and reached out his hand to the other. The other man, hesitantly, took a step back. Weapons raised on both sides of the clearing. Safety mechanisms were switched off, and sights were focused.

"The first man still stood with his hand outstretched, not flinching, and not caring that he was an easy target. Again, he extended his hand saying, 'Let the children play.' The second man stepped forward, taking his hand.

"They stood there for what must have seemed like an eternity, hand shaking hand, watching their children.

"The others, on both sides, not sure just what was going on, lowered their weapons. The two men slowly backed away from each other, then turned and walked back over to join their respective factions.

"'What happened out there?' they were asked. 'The old female.' They each told the story. 'She said to let the children play. She reminded me of my grandmother.' 'What old female?' they were heard to exclaim on both sides of the clearing. The two men turned, looking at each other across the clearing, both pointing at the place where she once stood. There was no one there.

The legend continues that all of the troops, on both sides, sat down on the grass that day in plain sight of each other, neither side showing any signs of aggression. They sat there watching the children play, cheering them on and encouraging them. They found that it wasn't what made them different that mattered, it was what they had in common that counted. The children showed them that.

"The men returned with their friends everyday and sat on opposite sides of the clearing, watching the children. They were caught completely off guard one day by a scouting contingent from a third faction who leveled their weapons at them, ready to discharge.

"'Let the children play,'" said one of the seated men. 'What?' asked the leader of the third faction. 'Are any of the children from your faction?' the seated man asked. 'Well yes, I recognize two of them.' he responded. Putting his free hand up to his mouth, the soldier was poised to call out to the children from his faction. He felt a hand touch his elbow. 'Wait,' the seated man said, 'let them play.' 'Yes, let them play,' echoed the group from the other side of the clearing.

"Everyone rose to his feet and walked to the center of the clearing where they all shook hands. The soldiers were perplexed. They weren't sure what to do. 'Join us,' said one of the men. 'Yes, sit with us and watch the game,' said another from the other side.

"The leader motioned, and his men reluctantly lowered their weapons.

"This, Mi-kal, was the beginning of the Resurrection!" Trr said proudly. "We have many statues that commemorate the event, and on the base of each of those statues are the words, 'Let the Children Play' as a constant reminder to us all as to what is truly important and what is mere folly."

"That was an excellent story!" I exclaimed, "And you tell it very well. I could actually see it in my mind!"

"Yes, Mi-kal, it is one of my favorite legends. I often told it to our children when on rotation. They loved it also."

"So, that's what happened to your god," I stated, "you just forgot about him."

"No, Mi-kal, it wasn't that easy. A couple of the surviving factions tried to hold on to the belief, but their religions slowly faded into what you would call 'myths.'

"After a couple of generations, they were regarded as little more than intriguing philosophical theories, and it was widely looked upon as incredible that anyone could have actually believed that the stories about the Keeper were true; much like the way people today look at the Greek 'myths,' about Zeus and Hera and their offspring."

"Earlier, you said that there was one officially recognized religion in your society. What is it?" I asked.

"Oh, so you remembered that!" Trr said, smiling. "Let me see...Mi-kal, it is often difficult to differentiate between religion and science on my world. Our religion changes as our scientific theories are revised. Although we are now relatively sure that our theories are correct, something occasionally surfaces that forces us to reevaluate and subsequently add to, subtract from, or even discard those theories that are affected by the newly discovered information."

"Give me an example of something that really changed one of your theories," I pressed him.

"Aha! I have the perfect example, Mi-kal, the trilyons!

"A few thousand years ago, while exploring one of the many semi-habitable spheres in another galaxy, one of our...explorers happened upon a unique sub-sentient life form that we later dubbed a trilyon. A trilyon looks a little like a cross between a soft rock and a lump of cheese, somewhat resembling a smooth sponge.

"At any rate, this explorer, Yon, placed four of them into a small bio-stasis chamber and brought them back to our sphere for research. However, much to Yon's surprise, when the chamber was opened, there were six trilyons inside. Yon double-checked his entry log, and sure enough, he had only recorded four specimens.

"The natural conclusion to draw was that they had somehow 'mated' and subsequently multiplied. This revelation sparked interest throughout the scientific community because the concept of living, breeding rocks was unheard of. A select group of scientists began to experiment with the trilyons carefully. They placed two of them on an examination table and coaxed them to mate. Nothing happened. After days of close, around-the-clock observation, the experiment was scrapped, and the two trilyons were put into a containment vessel. The next morning, however, when the container was opened, there were three trilyons inside!

"Once again, the lab became a blur of activity and theoretical suppositions. A clear container was placed on a table, and two more of the trilyons were placed inside. They watched carefully for hours, and again, nothing happened. Someone suggested that they turn down the lights and curtail conversation. Still, nothing happened.

"At last a scientist suggested that they cover the container. Sure enough, when the cover was removed a few minutes later, there were three identical trilyons inside. The excitement could be felt in the minds of citizens miles away from the facility. The experiments continued.

"Three trilyons were placed into the container. It was covered. Minutes later, when it was uncovered, five trilyons were inside. They were astonished!

"The next experiment saw six trilyons placed into a container, and nine were taken out. Without marking them, the original trilyons could not be distinguished from the new ones, and because no one was quite sure how they multiplied because they would never do it while being observed—even by a recording device—no one was ever sure which was which.

"Did they split in half? Did they both contribute to the third? Was it magic? Maybe it was some process that we just don't understand yet.

"At any rate, the trilyon experiments gave birth to a new system of mathematics. We fondly call it 'trithmatic.' One plus one no longer equaled two, it equaled three. Two is only found as the result of three minus one. Three plus one equals five, while two plus two equals six. As crazy as it sounds, it works, and one can only accurately count trilyons using trithmatic. Regular mathematics does not apply, and is always inaccurate, so the new trithmatic became an equally valid and logical system of counting.

"Well, know-it-all mathematicians, who believed that math, *real* math, was irrefutable, constant, and unchangeable, found themselves stymied. To acknowledge trithmatic was to admit fallibility.

"It was a tough pill to swallow, but after accreditation, all mathematic journals were amended to incorporate trithmatic."

"You really know how to trip me out, don't you, Trr?" I exclaimed. "Some of this stuff is just too unreal!"

"There are more exceptions then there are rules, dear Mi-kal," Trr quipped, "and one must remain open-minded to the antitruths if one is to grow in truth and knowledge."

"So that changed your religion?" I asked.

"That was merely an example of why our current belief systems are not considered sacred. We believe that one day, much of what we hold true today, will become trite, in light of some new revelation. Remember, however, that currently used knowledge is itself, the best avenue for the discovery of new knowledge. In other words, use what you have to build what you don't. The future feeds upon the past; it is shaped by it.

"Our religion has undergone many subtle changes over the aeons, but our basic belief has remained pretty much the same for the past four or five thousand years."

"Is the Keeper gone for good?" I asked.

"For the most part, yes, Mi-kal, but the Globe is still around in a more sophisticated theoretical sense. It is now believed to be comprised of solid force. Anything contacting this force is 'smashed' into its basic components. This includes light, sound, matter, and energy. The resulting refuse rebounds and is repelled back towards the center of the Globe, in its sub-atomic form, such as quarks, leptons, gluons and the like, as you call them. By the way, your theory of relativity may work for you now, but it is somewhat inaccurate, and adherence to it should not be allowed to hamper your future progress. Remember, nothing is sacred except the truth, and we are still searching for that ultimate truth.

"Now, back to my religion," Trr continued. "These particles are constantly aligning themselves with other particles as they continue on their journey back home, towards the center of the Globe, or universe. They take on the form of gasses and small bits of matter along the way. Many of these homeward-bound materials collide with or affect different bodies as they come into contact or proximity with them.

"Many times, depending upon the molecular makeup of the two interacting substances, chain reactions take place, which have repercussions on a cosmic scale. As your technology grows, and your ability to interface more accurately with the cosmos follows suit, your knowledge of these interactions will grow and ultimately change the way you see yourselves, your world, and your place in the universe.

"We believe that when substantial amounts of this matter and anti-matter, that is to say, when more of the universe, is making the trip inward, rather than outward, cosmological changes will occur on a universal scale.

"Large bodies of outwardly spiraling matter will be caught up in the waves of inwardly rushing substances, and the universe, as we know it, will begin to collapse and begin to feed upon itself as it rushes towards its center.

"When the forces at the center of the universe are substantial enough, and the energy levels reach a critical point, an explosion of inconceivable magnitude will occur, and once again reshape the universe.

"We believe that this is what created the universe we see today, and that many aeons from now, it will happen again. All things will be washed away, and created anew, even your God."

"So, everything and everyone is going to die?" I asked sullenly.

"Yes, in a sense," replied Trr. "Even death will die, but we believe that life will be born again."

"Then what's the point to all of this?" I asked desperately.

"The point is to make the journey the most wondrous, fulfilling, happiest, shared experience that we can. Just think, Mi-kal, we have *life!* Do you understand how precious that is? Do you not understand that being able to understand, to suppose, to contemplate, to communicate and to share the experience of being alive is in itself a miracle! This wonderful universe has blessed us with cognizance! Don't close your mind to it, revel in it. Rejoice because you can!"

"But how is life going to be reborn out of death?" I prodded.

"That is where our religion most distinguishes itself from our science, Mi-kal. We believe that it started with a wish. Understand me. Everything needed to make life possible is a constant in the universe. Water evaporates, but rain is possible because the basic elements are always preserved. Such is life. All of the elements will be preserved, perhaps in their most primitive form, but nevertheless, nothing is truly lost.

"One needs only to combine the proper ingredients in the proper order to bake a cake. So too did it take billions of years for even the most basic elements to join at the center of the universe.

But we believe that a kind of Cosmic Mind was born there, in the form of a wish. This Wish was a very primitive wish. It was a wish to be. To exist. And this Wish slowly became a Will to live. An expression of intent, in its most basic form. And this Will became a Need. Not just a want, but a need to express itself, like a yearning to be something, somewhere, somewhen, in some shape or form. And this Will, this Need, became like unto a Mind, a Mind with primitive ideas about expression. And this yearning, this need, this willful Mind, we believe, is what ultimately shaped the cosmos by causing the spark that ignited the ball at the center of the universe, sending this Force of creation, in pieces, across the heavens, to its new homes. And this Force, this creative power, directed by the Cosmic Mind, manifests itself in the life we see around us.

"There is no god above, Mi-kal, we, each of us, are the divine sparks of the cosmic fire we call life. Deep down inside, we all know this. All life is God, and God has no life save that which we collectively exhibit. And life's greatest triumph is the *love* of itself, as it appears in its many shapes and expressions throughout the universe."

"Now you've got me afraid to step on an ant!" I remarked.

"Don't be, Mi-kal. Life was meant to feed upon itself. The process of natural selection and, subsequently, the food chain is of divine creation. It was intended to be, to sustain life itself. If life did not consume other life, then life would cease to be.

"Our science has permitted us to minimize our absorption of other life forms, but we 'ate' much in the same way you do for millions of years. In fact, our children, during their formative or 'growing' years, still eat a balanced diet of living substances.

"Of course, no life should be taken for granted, but self-preservation will necessitate the swatting of a fly or mosquito, or the extermination of ants, before they bite you or infest your dwelling. With many larger forms of life, it becomes a matter of kill or be killed. One cannot reason with a grizzly bear or a rabid dog. Killing for the sake of killing is tragic, however.

"To hunt or scavenge for food is admirable, but to hunt purely for sport is an abomination. Lower life forms, those without higher cognizant reasoning faculties, or sentience, are expected to consume and be consumed by higher life forms. It is the way. It is natural, it is unavoidable.

"Let us also remember that plant life is exactly that, life. And although many of you humans choose to make a vast distinction between eating plant life and animal life, the plant makes no such distinction. It only understands, on a primitive level, that you are killing it. Hopefully, on some level, it also understands the necessity of your actions. After all, being a plant may not be much of a life, but it is all that a plant has. When a plant or animal sacrifices its life by being eaten, it contributes to the continuation of life. When humans die and are buried in coffins it shows an unwillingness to contribute anything back to the whole. It is taking but refusing to give."

"Well, what do you people do?" I sniped, "leave dead bodies lying around everywhere?"

"In a sense, yes," Trr replied. "Our physical remains are taken to a facility much like a high-tech mortuary, where the cause of death is certified, authenticated, and recorded. Next, all artificial and synthetic organs and limbs are removed, leaving only the organic remains, which are then, how do you say…emulsified."

"You grind up your dead bodies?" I exclaimed.

"You burn yours," he responded. "Mi-kal, cremating one's remains renders them all but useless to other life forms. We, on the other hand, break the remains down into a liquefied state, which is then spread throughout the forest and wildlife areas all over our sphere. Our bodies are composed of the organic materials we have absorbed from our world, and so, fittingly, we return those nutrients back to nature, where they are absorbed by new, or different, forms of life. We become part of the living world again, not part of the dead one."

"But what about Heaven? What about your soul? Do you just grind that up with the rest?" I asked sarcastically.

Trr hesitated. "That's a good question, Mi-kal. We have spent thousands of years trying to prove or disprove scientifically the occurrence of life after death. Our finest minds have philosophized and hypothesized about it, largely to no avail. The official scientific response is that the mind and spirit/soul cease to exist when the body ceases to function. This conclusion was not easily ascertained, however. It was the result of a great deal of extensive, and at times imaginative, research.

"Our 'scientific minds' tell us that death is the end. Our 'philosophical minds' and our hearts, keep insisting that death is but a new beginning.

"What were the experiments like?" I asked.

"There were many different types of experiments. Too many to elaborate on, but I will tell you of one of my favorites.

"Once there was scientist named Las. Las must have been somewhere around two thousand Earth years old, at the time, give or take a couple of centuries. Las knew he was dying, and no amount of replacement or enhancement surgery could correct the synaptical deterioration that his brain was suffering from.

"Las was somewhat of a philosopher also. He believed very strongly in the separation of body, mind, and spirit/soul. He loved to list the differences between them, so, on his behalf, I will briefly attempt to define them.

"The body is the physical self or the organic part of the being. Las, like many others, believed that someone who had lost his arms, legs, torso, eyes, lips, and ears but could still think, was just as much a person, and had just as much a right to be happy, as a being who retained all of the aforementioned parts. The body, then, is merely that which encases the real being, or person, as you would call it.

"The mind, a by-product of the brain, however, is considerably more important than the body. Las was fond of saying, 'You can change a being's body, but only he can change his mind.' The body is useless without the mind. It's like a lamp without a power source. No matter how beautiful it may be to look at, it serves no purpose save that of decoration. But the *mind*...! The mind can go places the body could never venture. It can do things the body could not endure. It can experience the nonexistent and ponder the unfathomable.

"The mind is divine, and should be cultivated and cherished, and treated with the utmost respect; to alter it by artificial means that may damage it is like throwing paint at your Mona Lisa, disfiguring it, and destroying its true value.

"The mind should be kept pristine, if one wishes to experience life and its wonderful variations. Anyone who knowingly or willingly jeopardizes the well-being of his or her mind, for recreational or experimental purposes, does not deserve to have it!"

I flashed back to Trr's experiments on me, and I began to grow apprehensive.

"I promised you that we would never cause you any permanent damage to your mind or body, Mi-kal, and we haven't. You may find that you have changed, but you have not been harmed. Please believe me."

I'm not quite sure why, but I did.

"I will continue, Mi-kal. The spirit/soul is a much trickier aspect of the self. We have one word for it, though you have two. The spirit is that which animates the body and the mind. The spirit is the life force itself. It can be described as the electricity that makes life work. Without the spirit, the mind would find no motivation to think, and the body would have no impetus to act. The spirit, or life force, intensifies or wanes depending upon the state of mind or emotion the being is experiencing. When excited, scared, or elated, the spirit shines brightly. When depressed, relaxed, or solemn, the spirit glows dimly. Many beings can read these fluctuations of the aura. Are you still with me, Mi-kal?"

"Yeah, go ahead," I said, trying to take it all in.

"The soul gives the spirit its drive. By this I mean that the spirit has no direction. The spirit is neither good nor bad, it is just there to act as a power source. The soul is what determines the goodness or badness of an entity. Right and wrong are concepts in the mind, which is governed by the soul, and powered by the spirit.

"In your culture, a zombie is a body with a spirit, but his mind is not governed by a soul. Thus, he is said to be soulless.

"When we say a person is lovable, kind, generous, or the opposite of those things, we are referring to the attributes of his soul, not his body, mind, or spirit. When we say that a person is funny, smart, wise, or their opposites, we are referring to the attributes of his mind. And when we say that a person is energetic, animated, lively, or their opposites, we are referring to his spirit. I hope I have made myself clear.

"The soul, then, is the measure of the being. We are born with a body that has certain potentials and limitations, but, by and large, we are hampered by those inherent limitations. Our minds, however, can be wonderfully broadened and enlightened, although our environment may well limit our understanding of the universe. The mind must be taught, and that teaching may or may not be flawed. But the spirit/soul is the 'true' us.

"We are ultimately judged by what kind of being we are. Whether we are tall or short, fat or thin, intelligent or ignorant, wise or foolish; whether we are quick or slow, or strong or weak, ultimately, none of those descriptions truly reflect the true 'inner us."

"If we are to become worthy of life, the ultimate gift, then let that life be measured by how much we love, and are loved, by others. Not out of fear, not out of obligation, but because we deserve to be loved for the person we are inside, despite our physical or mental prowess.

"Physical characteristics are fleeting. Mental abilities subside with time. But the spirit/soul, the fire and its conscience, will burn beyond this lifetime.

"Las believed this, but he also wished to know more. Where does the spirit/soul go when we die? Or is the flame snuffed out, as many would have us believe.

"Las made a decision to devote the final years of his life to answering this question. He found dying patients who were willing to undergo stringently controlled experiments at the time of their transition."

"Las was convinced that the spirit/soul was released from the mind/body at the moment of death. If this were true, he concluded, then it should be possible to trap the spirit/soul inside an airtight containment cylinder."

"In the first experiment, electrodes, oxygen valves, and feeding tubes were connected to the sealed tank and to the dying body. The scientists registered no aura or spiritual trace residues within the cylinder after the patient expired. These early failures did not, however, dissuade Las. The life support systems were all removed, because it was determined that if anything could be allowed into the containment cylinder, then via the same avenue, something could escape out of it.

"The new experiments had little better results. All of the new monitoring devices registered a cessation of all bodily functions, including thought, respiration, heartbeat, and neural impulses. The spirit/soul had to be going somewhere, Las thought, but where, and why couldn't they observe its departure?

"Las reached the conclusion that his experiments were failing for two reasons. First, the containment cylinders, no matter how solid, did permit the functions of the body to be monitored and measured by outside instruments. He realized that this was possible because, obviously, light, sound, thought, and vibrational waves were all escaping through the walls of the cylinder. It was true that solids, gasses and liquids could not escape, but it was equally true that wavelengths could enter and exit, almost at will.

How does one trap a wavelength? That was the question.

"The second problem, Las surmised, was the unwillingness of the subjects to wait around long enough to attempt any effort to communicate. Maybe they just weren't trying hard enough. Maybe something irresistible was drawing them away. Maybe they just didn't know how, any more than a newborn knows how to speak the language of its new world. What to do?

"Well, first of all, Las, with his failing health, devised and constructed an energy field containment chamber, which emitted dangerous levels of a rare form of radiation. Any vibration or wavelength attempting to pass through this energy field would be prohibited, measured, and monitored by a group of intrepid scientists who, by putting their lives in jeopardy, would attempt to capture the moment in their minds and on their instruments."

"Unfortunately, the long hours and exposure to minute levels of radiation only hastened Las' impending death. One morning, when the other scientists arrived at the laboratory, they found Las lying inside the containment chamber. They instantly knew what was expected of them. Their equipment was tested and retested for accuracy. Every conceivable precaution was taken so that no amount of error could taint the results. This was it, the final experiment of their esteemed colleague, Scientist Las.

"Six hours, thirty seven minutes, and fifteen seconds after their arrival, Las' heartbeat ceased. The containment field automatically surged to maximum, and the laboratory lights dimmed to near-total blackness.

"The only glow in the room was coming from inside the containment field. What happened next is still being debated today. The two scientists who survived for the following three days both repeated the same story, over and over.

"These two scientists claimed that they had witnessed Las' spirit/soul separate itself from his body. It floated for a moment and then attempted to pass out of the containment field, only to be jolted back into its center. Again and again it tried to escape, with increasing effort, only to be rebuffed. The spirit/soul began to glow ever more brightly as it banged itself against the field, which began to hum menacingly.

"Suddenly, there was an explosion, catching everyone off guard and slamming the scientists into the instruments and walls of the lab. Fires broke out, and radiation levels skyrocketed. The entire building was evacuated and sealed off.

"A special contingent of rescue specialists, wearing heavy anti-radiation garments, were allowed in, to search for survivors. The two scientists were rushed to a special facility and placed inside radiation-proof cubicles. In their agonizing, pain-racked, delusional state, they told their story over and over to whomever would listen to them. Everyone was assured that the scientists' accounts could not be relied upon, due to the massive brain damage and radiation poisoning each had sustained. They both died babbling incoherently, within hours of each other, on the third day.

"No one could ever prove the truth or falsity of their account, but it was never argued that something had indeed transpired inside the laboratory that day. All the records were destroyed in the explosion and ensuing fire, and nothing, due to contamination, was allowed to be removed from the building. The experiment was permanently banned, along with the rare radioactive isotopes used in the experiment. The building itself was covered with several layers of radiation containment materials and then coated with a heavy layer of lead-based stone, much like your concrete. Eventually, this was turned into a monument, pyramidal in shape, that bears a plaque that reads, 'In Memory of Las and Those Who Gave Their Lives in the Pursuit of the Ultimate Truth. We Salute You!' Of course, this is only a rough translation."

I sat there, awed by the story Trr had just told me when I was suddenly wrenched back to reality by the glaring eyes of Zwig and Gnar, who were now standing to my left. Their stares shifted to Trr, who, in turn, glared back. I heard him inside my head telling them that he had not told me too much and that they should return to their duties. Then silence. I could not hear their replies.

Again, Trr was in my mind, saying that he didn't tell them how to conduct their encounters and that he did not appreciate their interference. Silence again. Then Trr, touching my arm, said—half asking, half insisting—"Why don't you step into the dream machine, Mi-kal? There is a program I'd like you to experience that I'm sure you'll enjoy." Without comment, I did as he asked.

As the cover grew dark I could see Trr to my left, programming a panel. He turned to Zwig and Gnar and silently continued their conversation.

In the darkness, I couldn't help but wonder what they were saying. I wondered what had gone wrong, and how it was going to effect me. The program Trr had called up demanded my attention, and my thoughts were, once again, sequestered by the dream machine.

This will be my final attempt to dissuade those of you who consider yourselves devout adherents to any given faith to discontinue reading this book.

I don't know what else to say. I'm not sorry that I felt compelled to write this story, but I do apologize for any discomfort that reading it may cause.

Chapter Eight

Revelations (The Antitruth)

The program that Trr had wanted me to see was somewhat of a continuation of his last story. It seems that, although Las' experiments were never continued, no attempt was made to duplicate them due to an imposed ban on all unsanctioned radiation-based experiments. The theorists, philosophers and scientists had a field day drawing hypotheses and rewriting probability theorems.

They finally agreed on a theory that, though vague, was nonetheless enlightening. It seems that the spirit/soul releases from the mind/body at the moment of death. The spirit/soul itself is a force of nature that, just as helium or steam must rise, or sound waves must resonate, must emanate outwardly to rejoin the cosmic life force once released. The compulsion to do this, it is theorized, is perhaps the most powerful compulsion known to any being, even stronger than the compulsion to feed, to sleep, or to mate.

It isn't clear what drives this compulsion, but it is also theorized that the spirit/souls that are not prepared to make this journey often fight this compulsion and attempt to remain in the physical realm rather than succumb to the spiritual one.

Once ascendance takes place, it is believed, the spirit/soul dissipates, or loses it's selfness to the whole of the cosmic life force. All semblance of individuality is absorbed, and becomes one with the All. It is best described as a raindrop falling into the ocean. The raindrop becomes part of every wave on every shore, part of every glass of water, and of every future rainfall.

So too does the spirit/soul find a godlike status within the Cosmic Life force.

Every new life draws its spirit/soul from this source and surrenders itself once again to the Whole, when it releases anew. Life on every sphere, and in every outreach of the universe, shares in this common life force, making us all *one* with each other and kin to the very universe itself.

Of course, none of this has been proven, but neither has it been disproven.

As the program ended, I found myself compelled to sleep. I'm not sure if I was truly sleepy or if Trr had planned this as part of the dream machine's programming.

While asleep, I had a dream that was reminiscent of a story I had once concocted for a philosophy class to explain the dubiousness of faith-based religions. Bear with me.

God is really a Bunny Rabbit. A very large rabbit, who hops around the world so fast that the human eye cannot see Him. We know that He exists, because if He stopped hopping, there would be nothing to keep the Earth spinning. Subsequently, it would stop turning, which would result in one side of the Earth baking, while the other side would freeze, resulting in the end of life on our planet.

Thank goodness the Bunny loves us. Praise the Bunny! At

times, the Bunny hops too fast, causing hurricanes or tornadoes. At times, He comes down too hard, causing earthquakes or tidal waves. His breath becomes the clouds in the sky, and He uses his ears to punch holes in the clouds, causing it to rain down upon the waiting Earth, watering our crops and quenching our thirst.

If one leads a worthy life, then when one dies, the Bunny Rabbit bounces one's soul up to heaven on His broad-shouldered back. If one leads an unworthy life, the Bunny descends upon your soul, pounding it down to hell. It is my advice that you behave yourself because the Bunny may be watching.

The point of the story is that with all of the experiential criteria I have given you, my Bunny must necessarily exist to explain all of the aforementioned phenomena. In other words, how can you doubt my Bunny so long as the Earth turns and the rain falls? It is impossible to disprove the existence of the Bunny because we have no logical explanation for why things happen the way they do. Sure, science can predict or explain what occurs, and the apparent causes, but not why things happen to work in such an orderly manner. My Bunny provides that order and stability, and you cannot prove that He doesn't.

In my dream, the Bunny was coming for me, although I woke up before I could learn my ultimate fate.

When I woke up, the cover of the dream machine was clear again. I could see Trr, Gnar, and Zwig engaged in what appeared to be a heated debate. I couldn't hear them, but for the first time, they were using body language to express themselves as they thought-transferred.

I tapped on the cover of the dream machine to alert them that I was finished, to no avail. I did this repeatedly, but they appeared to be too caught up in their conversation to pay me any attention. I must admit, at this point claustrophobic tendencies started to rise in me. I was about to panic. I took a wild guess that there had to be a switch or a button inside somewhere that would open the damned-thing. I felt around the edges until I found something. It was a box-shaped square, with raised lines on it, underneath the edge of the padding inside the machine. I pushed a square, but nothing happened, then another and another. It was then that the cover went black, and I was assaulted with the most intense onslaught of images, both before me and inside my mind, that I had ever been subjected to inside the dream machine.

This program wasn't meant for me. The language must have been their language, because it was unlike any I had ever heard before. But I didn't need the words to understand clearly what I was seeing. I was privy to an alien account of very specific events, laid out in a journalistic manner, chronicling direct interaction between Trr's people and human beings.

Although the images passed very quickly, I had no problem keeping up with or understanding the story they told.

This is the story of Imman.

It appears that several thousand years ago, Trr's people were allowed to interact with humans on a limited basis. Repeated attempts had been previously made to influence humans by forcing them to adhere to the guidelines set forth by the "gods," as they were believed to be. This involvement took place on a global scale, with the "gods" demanding loyalty and strict adherence to their own codes of ethics. When the humans failed to comply, they were punished, sometimes severely.

I saw things I will never forget. I witnessed an incident where several spacecraft were organized to change the atmospheric conditions in a region, causing it to rain continuously, until floods destroyed large populations of people.

I saw scenes of spacecrafts firing beams of energy down upon those who I understood to be the Israelites of centuries past. I watched as some of the disobedient were disintegrated where they stood, reduced to dehydrated mounds upon the earth. The stories were familiar ones.

I saw repeated attempts to "encourage" leaders to persuade their people to obey the edicts of the "gods" and how they were made slaves as punishment for their refusal to comply.

I saw those same Israelites freed by the Egyptians after they saw their own people mercilessly slaughtered for failure to submit to the wishes of that region's "God on high." I witnessed spacecraft using matter displacement energy waves to part the waters, only to shut them off in time to facilitate the escape of the fleeing Israelites.

I saw them use holographic imaging and laser beams to inscribe their new commandments upon the tablets. I witnessed Moses taken aboard a spacecraft as his people entered into the promised land.

The gods were allowed to rule with an iron fist for centuries, until reports of their atrocities reached their native planet, and the word was sent down to cease and desist.

A new order of gods was dispatched to Earth, and the old order was recalled. According to a brief entry, they were punished for their crimes by voluntarily undergoing extended counseling and agreeing to the revocation of their credentials.

The "new gods" set out to spread their influence in different ways. Because direct intervention was now forbidden, clever ways of bending the rules by indirect influence were devised. This is one such story I watched in detail and disbelief.

A woman who was engaged to be married, was selected for artificial insemination. A genetic implant was introduced into her womb, which carried the genes of one of the local "gods." The impregnation of the egg she carried produced a hybrid of the two species. Due to reasons which were not made clear, the wedding was postponed, which led to the discovery, by the groom-to-be that the woman was already pregnant, although she insisted that she was still a virgin and that "angels" had recruited her to carry the son of God.

Her husband-to-be was appalled and could not decide whether to hide her away or to abandon her. The "angels" intervened and assured him, in a dream, that the child was of divine creation, and not the result of infidelity. This reinforced the woman's story, so the man left his home with the woman, and they traveled to a distant city. We know these people as Joseph and Mary, although these are not the names they were called by. The city was Bethlehem.

On the night of the impending birth of the baby Imman, as the gods called him, his biological father's spacecraft hovered high above the birth site to record the event. They made no attempt to conceal themselves; in fact, they marked the event by causing their spacecraft to glow so intensely it could be seen from many miles away in all directions. This was, after all, a momentous occasion of the highest magnitude. A baby was being born, half human, half god!

The baby Imman was not abandoned by the gods. Quite the contrary. He was regularly schooled and taught many of the mind techniques of his celestial father. Among this instruction was levitation, telekinesis, telepathy, and, most importantly, healing through psychic transmission—the laying on of hands. This did not work for all afflictions, but when aided by medications given him by his father, "miracles" could be performed.

Imman was an excellent student. He learned quickly and was of the proper temperament to succeed in the most important, long-awaited part of his father's plan.

Imman was told that he would have to die a painful death, but not to worry, for he would be reborn. Imman was skeptical. Along with his reassurances, his father gave him the instruments he would require for his resurrection, and sent him to carry out their plan.

Still skeptical, Imman tested the drugs, first on a little girl, who was given a minimal dosage, and successfully revived, and later to his friend Lazarus.

As expected, the first drug placed the individual in a coma, or deathlike state, from which they could not be awakened for three days. Their heartbeat and respiration were lowered to almost undetectable levels. This drug was very similar to the one the space travelers took when placing themselves into stasis for long intergalactic journeys.

The second drug was similar to smelling salts, and was used, if needed, to bring a person fully back to consciousness much quicker than waiting for the first drug to wear off.

Imman surrounded himself with unknowing disciples, who were told only what they needed to know, which usually consisted mainly of the gospel he preached.

Despite their methods, I was convinced that these galactic intruders only had our best interest at heart. They seemed to share a genuine concern, even love, for the people of Earth. And I certainly cannot find much fault with the teachings they gave Imman to pass on to us. Imman was indeed of divine creation, and his efforts were heroic ones.

Although no one was told the entire plan, Imman did need quite a bit of aid to reach his goal successfully. His closest and most trusted confidant was Judas, his treasurer. Imman was no fool. It was his practice to look into the hearts and minds of his followers, and he knew Judas to be worthy.

The plan was drawn in such a way as to adhere closely to the holy scriptures and prophesies given to the Jews hundreds of years earlier. If that meant riding into town on a donkey, then so be it.

After performing many miraculous feats of healing, raising the dead, and walking on water, it became evident that Imman was not going to win over the hearts and minds of the Jewish people. This necessitated that they begin the second part of the plan.

Imman arranged to have himself crucified. He appealed to one of the Pharisees, Caiaphas, to convince the others that he must die on the cross. He arranged for a private burial site, belonging to a follower, so that he might be secretly taken away. He discussed his impending fate with Judas and instructed him that upon his signal, he must go to the chief priest and betray him. Judas tried repeatedly to change Imman's mind, but could not. Instead, Imman convinced him that it was his duty to obey, as one of his disciples, telling him, "When I give you the sign, it will be time for you to do my bidding."

It is important to remember that Imman knew, days in advance, that the Jews wanted to see him dead. He had promised them resurrection if they would but believe in him, but even Lazarus' resurrection was not enough to overshadow Imman's blatant attempts to give the God and covenant of the Jews to the Gentiles. They would never forgive him for that.

Nevertheless, Imman had more than enough time to abandon his plan and to leave his encampment to avoid arrest, if he had so desired. But Imman was there to be crucified, and although he still had his doubts he trusted in his father's word.

When Imman was ready, he gave Judas the sign by dipping his bread into his bowl. Though some accounts state that they were told that Judas would betray Imman, it was in truth, known only after the fact, which is why, first of all, no one attempted to detain Judas, and secondly, Judas knew exactly where Imman would go with his disciples after he left the supper.

In Judas' defense, no man kills himself for betraying someone he dislikes or doesn't believe in. He killed himself because he could no longer face the others or the impending fate of his close friend Imman after the coerced betrayal.

After he was arrested, Imman remained defiant in the face of authority. He never recounted or asked for them to spare his life.

While hanging on the cross, Imman called out to a man in the crowd who rushed to him and gave him a drink of the medication. Imman cried out to his father and slumped over in a deathlike state.

Although it was customary to leave the crucified on the cross for several days, Imman was taken down almost immediately, during a downpour created by his father, and after his wounds were bound, was taken away to his prearranged burial place. On the third day, as planned, his father and an associate drugged the guards and removed his son from the tomb. He was taken to the spacecraft where he was revived, administered medication and the very best medical care, and sent back to his disciples as proof of the resurrection.

Believing them finally to be convinced, Imman's father raised him up into the spacecraft, where he sat at his father's right hand, and witnessed what he had wrought.

Imman returned with his father to his father's planet, where he died a few years later. Because of his mixed heritage, Imman was never truly accepted as an equal among his father's brethren, although he was held in high esteem for his great sacrifices on his father's behalf. Imman never married or conceived offspring.

The program ended, the cover returned to its transparent state, and I looked out into the room where all three of my hosts were quietly going about their tasks.

I banged on the cover this time, which caused them all to look up simultaneously. As the cover began to slide open, I stepped out of the dream machine and headed for the portal. All three of them were staring at me intently, when Gnar suddenly glanced over at the panel beside the dream machine. I'm not sure what he saw there, but it caused him to cry out first in his own language, and then again in English, "Stop him you must. He knows!"

"You can't stop me," I snapped. "You don't have the right to stop me."

"We *do* have the right to stop you, Mi-kal," Trr said sternly. "You cannot leave yet. We must talk."

"I'm tired of talking!" I rebuffed. "I'm outta here!" At least I thought I was, but they were holding me, restraining me with their minds.

"Please allow me to explain some things to you, Mi-kal," Trr said pleadingly. "Things you'll want to know."

What choice did I have? "Trr," I said, "I think I've already learned enough about you and your underhanded manipulative ways. I think I can fill in the blanks on my own! Your people have been screwing around with us for thousands of years, with your sadistic methods of control, trying to make us believe you were gods. You had no right to treat us that way. We would have made it on our own, without your so-called divine intervention. We didn't ask for your help, and we don't want it now, so why don't you all pack up your damned equipment and get the hell off of my planet!"

"Because we can't," Trr answered. "Your Jesus was not the only one of his kind. Similar experiments were performed all over your planet. Buddha, Mohammed, Vishnu, and many other great religious leaders were of our making, or the direct products of our inspirational tutelage. Think about it, Mi-kal, who do you truly believe aided in the construction of the pyramids? Who do you think sat on Mount Olympus and hurled lightning bolts? Who sat on the mountain tops of Tibet, doling out wisdom. Who inscribed their art work on the mountainsides of South America? Who constructed Stonehenge, and why? Who sunk Atlantis, and gave birth to Hercules and Samson? Who spliced the genes of the Minotaur and Pegasus? Why does practically every culture on Earth attempt to explain, in its own primitive way, how they were visited by the gods, who spoke to them and walked among them? This, Mi-kal, is an antitruth. You've always known it, deep down inside, but you've never accepted it.

"Go back and reread your Bible, read the Greek and Roman

myths, read the Koran, look into Taoism, read the ancient literature of a thousand cultures around the globe, like that of your Native Americans, we will be there, described in their words, and molded into their own peculiar belief systems. Could people everywhere on the face of the Earth have simultaneously been delusional? Of course not! Either you believe that all of your ancestors were fools, or that the gods they spoke of existed. Do not blame them for their child-like descriptions or depictions of a science that they could not even hope to comprehend. What is a spacecraft, to a man who has never seen a car, a flying chariot? What is a man wearing a jet pack on his back, floating above the crowd, an angel? How do you explain the holographic projection of a man's face, or of cool fire, as acts of God?

Why do people on every continent bow their heads and pray or meditate? Who will hear them, and why have they persisted throughout history? Who were the great sacrifices made to? Was everyone crazy, Mi-kal? Was everyone so foolish as to believe these so-called fantasies? I think not. Perhaps the benefit of the doubt should go to those who, like yourself, sought enlightenment.

"No, we are not truly 'gods,' but we were treated that way, and perhaps, in retrospect, we should have behaved differently. At the time, we did what we felt was best. When your civilizations were in their infancy, we treated you like unruly children, physically punishing you and making many of you pain-filled examples of disobedience. As those civilizations matured, so too did our disciplinary tactics. The more sophisticated you became, the more passive was our influence. Parents must learn when to let go, but good parents never totally abandon their children."

"Screw you, Trr. We're not your damned children. Your children are being hatched on some planet, somewhere in another galaxy. Where do you get off thinking you've been anointed guardians of the little man? You can take your self-righteousness and cram it! You have enough of our blood on your hands! You've been bathing in it for centuries!"

Trr grew silent. Turning, he faced Zwig and Gnar. They spoke silently for twenty or thirty seconds, until Trr turned to face me again. "Sit down, Mi-kal," he said, "you may as well hear the rest of it."

Chapter Nine

Drops

I really didn't feel like sitting down. I was nervous, fidgety, wired, and a host of other anxious emotions. I just wanted to get the hell out of there, or wake up from this nightmare.

Maybe I was afraid to hear anymore. Maybe I'd just had enough, and needed time alone to think about it. Maybe there was a part of me that had to listen, a part of me that needed to know. A frightened little part of me that wasn't going to be able to sleep at night unless I finished this thing. "Okay," I said. "Let's get this over with so I can go home."

Trr glanced over at Gnar and Zwig. They nodded, and, looking me in the eyes, Trr began.

"Remember the story I told you about my species, and our brush with extinction?" I nodded yes. "Well, Mi-kal, there is a side to that story that we are even less proud of.

"Many of our species had been exposed to radiation levels of differing degrees. Some suffered the obvious burns and disfigurement that accompany exposure. Others were affected in more subtle ways.

"During the Resurrection, there was a persistent problem with many of our children who were being born. Some were physically deformed, while others suffered mental impediments that rendered almost useless large portions of their brains.

"Although many generations had passed on our new sphere, and beautiful cities had been constructed, our facilities were filled with thousands of individuals who, due to no fault of their own, were 'societally dysfunctional.'

"Those with physical deformities, or handicaps, were the easiest to aid. The technology we brought with us allowed us to repair many of their afflictions surgically. However, their offspring were often born with similar problems that only exacerbated the situation.

"Although, due to their genetic impurity, the physically disadvantaged only had a life expectancy of forty or fifty Earth years, this was long enough to prolong the problem. The mentally impaired, however, had considerably longer life spans.

"We attempted to absorb or integrate them into the mainstream of our society, but they were unable to perform many of the more exacting tasks set before them. Slowly but surely, these individuals were relegated to menial employment status, where they performed most of the physical labor.

"As the need for physical labor diminished, many of them were regarded as dregs upon society, and spurned.

"Their children became the brunt of insults and prejudice. The adults were slowly reduced to an unenviable position in society, not unlike that of a slave.

"Because the mentally handicapped were unable to thought transfer, levitate, or defend themselves against psychic manipulation, their only defense was a physical one, and somewhat justifiably, they became violent.

"It became commonplace to find them in the counseling facilities by the thousands. Finally, they were rounded up and placed together in camps, not unlike your current reservations, where they were denied many of their previously held freedoms. They responded, finally, in the only way they knew: they revolted.

"The revolution was a short one. Although they were physically more than a match for the general populace, mentally even a small child could be taught to disable one of them with a psychic assault. Ambush tactics were employed, and brutal massacres would take place on a regular basis."

"Finally, a truce was called. Several leaders of the revolt met with the Assembly and demanded their rights and their freedom.

"After a great deal of debate, it was agreed upon that liberty for the mentally disadvantaged was a virtual impossibility in our society, and so the decision was made to find a new home for them.

"Several very distant planets were found to be suitable for life. Earth was among them. Scout ships were dispatched to ready the drop sites on the different continents. Quite often this meant eliminating other 'hostile' life forms that were already present. This was done using many different techniques, depending upon the size and intelligence quotient of the species. Some were almost human themselves.

"This is a very ugly part of our history, Mi-kal, but one we felt was necessary. We had to enhance the prospects of survival for our species, even if it meant the elimination of another. We slaughtered them by the thousands. Many of them retreated deep into hiding in the jungles and forests. As long as they stayed there, they were spared.

"Drops were made on several different continents in several different hemispheres to enhance the chances of survival and to make certain that no single disaster would devastate the entire population.

"It was decided that to survive in this new environment the new inhabitants would have to learn to use the resources available to them there, on the new planet. Any use of our superior technology was discouraged because it was felt that, in the long run, it would only hamper their adaptation to their new environment, although nutritional supplements were provided for many years.

"Each major drop site had a team of 'Overseers,' assigned to it. Life for the 'Earthmen' was difficult, and peace was fleeting. Splinter groups separated themselves from the drop sites and moved off to form new encampments in caves, forests, and crudely designed hovels. Although the Overseers attempted to remain in close contact with all of them, it became increasingly difficult.

"One of the promises made to these new Earthmen was that upon their deaths, their bodies would be lifted up and eventually returned to their home world, where they would be given a traditional burial and so rejoin the cycle. For this purpose, each of them was fitted with a kind of homing device, placed under the skin, so that no matter where they migrated, their bodies could later be retrieved and taken back up into the heavens, to be with their forefathers.

"By the third generation, this was becoming nearly impossible to do. First of all, their numbers, which grew very slowly at first, began to grow rapidly in the second hundred years of occupation. Also, the physiological and organic makeup of their offspring changed with every generation, due to their new environment and their intake of Earth substances. Taking their bodies back to our sphere threatened to contaminate our environment with their new diseases, so the burial process was performed on Earth by the Overseers, and a few generations later, it was abandoned altogether. At this point the people of Earth conceived of new and original ways of burying their dead—still clinging, however, to many of the spiritual and religious beliefs of their ancestors.

"Life expectancy for the initial 'drops' was approximately three hundred to nine hundred Earth years, due to the medical and dietary aid provided by the Overseers, but that expectancy declined rapidly as the Earthmen moved away and out into the hostile environment.

"The 'Elders' tried diligently to pass down the stories of their heritage to their children from one generation to the next, but like the retelling of any story, something gets lost and other things added in the narration. After a while, the stories were as much a product of Earth as they were of home.

"A very unfortunate trend surfaced after most of the Elders had passed away. Neighboring tribes, as you call them, would occasionally return to the drop sites to loot them. Quite often these excursions would become bloody ones, necessitating the development of better methods of defense. Quite often this meant the development of new, more effective weapons.

"The Overseers found themselves in the unique position of recording, for the first time, the actual primitive beginnings of civilization. If not interfered with, the Earthmen became adept at discovering and inventing new methods and tools to accomplish almost any task confronting them. Many of these accomplishments were later modified and enhanced with our own technology on our home planet. But the collection of raw ideas, and their applications, caused a major stir in our own scientific communities. We were literally watching ourselves recreate ourselves.

"Unfortunately, we were also watching ourselves destroy ourselves, and it was this overwhelming threat that prompted us to 'interfere,' as you call it. Without a resurgence of ethical and moral behavior, mankind was doomed to extinction. You were becoming better at solving the problems of defense then you were the problems of living together in harmony.

"You were truly brothers, in the literal sense of the word, but you were behaving as if you belonged to different species. Nowhere on Earth did any animal delight in killing one another the way humans did. All over the Earth, violence and tribalism became the only standards by which you seemed to live. You were our children, all of you, and you were destroying yourselves. We had to do something to stop you. We *had* to intercede.

"At first, our guidance was rejected. We became targets ourselves. The more generations that passed, the less you looked like us, and in time, each other. Your prospective environments and diets had changed you, until you failed to see how much alike you were and began to focus on the trivial differences.

"Bigotry and hatred were fanned by failures to communicate. Different languages and customs had separated you and drove you to distrust each other. What would you have us do, Mi-kal, pack up and go home? Abandon the mess we'd made?

"When my ancestors had returned to their original planet after the Resurrection, they found carnage, the likes of which you could not believe. Desperate people had taken to desperate measures to survive. They never realized that the only hope they had was to work together to salvage their world, and so they slaughtered one another, fighting over the scarce remaining resources on the planet. Eventually, it is believed, that the last of them died of radiation poisoning. The old world had been abandoned, but we took an oath as a people, never again to abandon our species."

"You see, we *cannot* leave until your survival is ensured. At the present time, the survival of your species is, like you said, in the hands of a few of your egotistical and power-hungry leaders. Pray that they do not strain the muscles of their authority by flexing them in the faces of the less advantaged. If someone were to call their bluff, would they respond? And would that response bring back the nightmare of your distant ancestors? Pray, Mi-kal. Pray to the Life force within us all, for the wisdom it will take to get you past this place in history and catapult you all into a brighter future of harmonious coexistence and joy.

"United, there is nothing you cannot accomplish, but divided by the silly tenets of nationalism, race, religion, color, and tribalism, you are forever teetering on the brink of disaster.

"It is time for the human race to grow up. It is time for you to reclaim your heritage as brothers, with one language, one world government, one religion, and one shared goal of preserving your world, and living in peace."

I didn't know what to say. It all made too much sense. Trr's account of human history sounded truer than any of the theories of evolution or divine creation stories I had ever heard before. The truth I had been taught seemed tenuous and fraught with inconsistencies. Trr's words made sense and pulled everything together. This was the Antitruth. That which stands against the together. This was the Antitruth. That which stands against the truth and defies denial.

"Everything you've told me *sounds* true," I said to Trr. "The evidence is overwhelming. I guess you have just as much right to be here as we do. I understand now why you did what you did.

"I promise to give these things a lot of thought, and perhaps, one day, I will share this Antitruth with others. I don't know how they'll take it, but then, I'm not sure I've got it all straightened out in my own head yet. You could have fabricated this whole thing to gain my confidence." At this, Trr shook his head softly.

"I know this is probably the last time I will see you, and I want to thank you for all that you have shared with me. I don't fear you any longer, and it's good to know that if there isn't a God overhead looking down on us with concern, at least someone is. Thanks again."

"You cannot leave yet, Mi-kal," Trr said in a strange voice. Zwig and Gnar nodded in agreement. "We cannot permit you to repeat this to anyone. Your world is not ready to know the Antitruth yet."

"What do you mean?" I asked, backing away. "I mean, if you don't want me to tell anyone, I won't, I swear it!" I was lying, and they knew it.

"We are sorry, Mi-kal, but you must get back into the psychovideographer."

"Why?" I asked in desperation. Why did you tell me all of this if you didn't want me to know it?"

"Because I needed to tell it, and you needed to hear it, Mi-kal. Even if you cannot remember, traces of it will stay with you and influence you in the future. You are better off for having heard it, and we, for having told it; the burden is lifting."

I was still backing away from them, and they kept slowly following me around the room.

"Can't we compromise on this, or something?" I asked as I bolted towards the closed portal.

"No," said Trr. "I am sorry that we cannot. Good night, Mikal."

As the world began to go black, I recall thinking over and over, "I will remember. I will remember. I will remember...." The last words I heard before sleep overcame me, however, were not my own. They belonged to Trr. He said, like a whisper in my mind, "I know."

Chapter Ten
The Wish

Are you still with me, Pat?

By the way, there was a ten-year gap between the time I wrote the first half of this book and the second. I'm not sure why it took me so long to finish it, it just seemed that every time I went to pick it up, something distracted me, and I'd shove it back under the bed. But it's finished now!

I think.

What amazes me most is that the dreams—and I'm about seventy-five percent sure that they were, in fact, dreams—are practically as clear to me today, as they were ten or twelve years ago. I haven't had any more since then, thank goodness. Only peace of mind, and a different grasp of reality.

I got something else from the dreams also: a renewed sense of hope for humanity. I firmly believe now, that together we can achieve virtually anything.

If we'd spend less time on "one-upmanship" and divert our resources towards common goals, we could eradicate world hunger, cure any and all diseases, and raise the standard of living for every man, woman, and child on the planet. The only thing stopping us is the artificial divisions we have placed between us. But these are walls that we can tear down, and together, we can touch this world with love and understanding. We can make it anything we want it to be, even paradise.

Who can stop us besides us? No one. No animal on Earth can stop us from making this heaven. We have the means. We lack the trust and the dedication.

If we could only learn to communicate with one another on a human level, rather than a monetary one, we would all benefit. There is no reason why everyone can't have a home, a job, and food on the table. These things are easy to fix, we just have to find people who are willing to fix them for the good of everyone, instead of people who are only interested in how much profit they can make for themselves and their wealthy friends.

People have been killed for telling lesser truths, but it's time we stood up and took responsibility for the state our world is in. We can no longer tolerate crime and the drug abuse that fuels much of it. We can no longer put up with laziness and an unwillingness to contribute something positive to society. We can no longer tolerate those people who want to contribute nothing more than starving ignorant children to an overburdened society. Birthrates must be held in check until we can provide a better environment to raise our children in.

No one wants to see his own part in the destruction of our world. No one wants to take the responsibility to do the difficult things needed to correct our inadequacies. We can all point fingers at the problems, but we refuse to give up even a little of our time, money, effort, or freedoms to achieve solutions to those problems.

We deserve the world we have. We are, by our apathy, supporting the antisocial behavior of the few and ensuring the collapse of the moral fabric that sustains civilization. We are not free to destroy our society, either individually or collectively. We inherited a pretty decent world from our forefathers, but we lack the courage and the fortitude to ensure that generations to come live lives filled with peace and brotherhood, rather than the turmoil and bigotry we now face on a day-to-day basis.

Will we permit this to be our epitaph, "They never really gave a damn about anything, not even themselves"?

Is this the lesson we are teaching our children? "Anything is acceptable, as long as you don't get caught"? What ever happened to integrity? What happened to righteousness and morality? What happened to make us so cynical and self-destructive?

Why do we insist on owning handguns, drinking alcohol, taking drugs, making cars that are unsafe or travel at speeds exceeding eighty miles per hour? Why do we support prostitution, gambling, and decadence? Why do we tolerate ridiculous prices, conspicuous consumption, and gluttony?

When is enough, enough? When do we say No more! to pornography, vandalism, and ignorance?

When will the brighter days begin? The days each of us secretly long for in our hearts?

Maybe they will begin when we find ourselves up against the wall. Maybe those brighter days are just around that corner down the block. Maybe our way is fraught with the dangerous threats of the vermin among us who are selling our souls for their profit. Maybe the brighter days are setting, in a future filled with nightmarish scenes from the reality we call now. Maybe this is all some horrible dream our society is dreaming.

We can choose to ignore the cracks in the foundation of our society and of our world. We have become adept at focusing on the positive, while ignoring the negative. Once upon a time, those cracks were small ones, and hardly worth the notice, so we stepped over them on our way to a brighter tomorrow. But those cracks have become chasms, and they threaten to swallow whole the best of us.

If we allow ourselves the freedom of apathy, then we will find ourselves the slaves of decadence.

Most of us can remember when it was safe to walk our streets, Most of us remember when we didn't have to lock our doors, and we knew and trusted our neighbors. What has happened to us? Have we given in to the worst of us and become prisoners, out on the streets with a day pass in our own neighborhoods? Should we have to fear for the lives of our children every time we turn our backs? What about our children? Who are they? They are not the children that we were. We have given them material things to try to make up for the morals and ethics we seem unsuited to pass on to them. Do we allow them to have the things they want, at the expense of the things they truly need, like a future, and a world fit to live in?

When will we take responsibility for our households and what we will permit inside them? The raunch we call entertainment, the nudity, the profanity, the violence and the callousness are slowly poisoning our minds by desensitizing our revulsion and demoralizing our emotions.

Is this what we are teaching our children? Is this the example we wish for them to follow? We are what we experience. What are our children experiencing? When will we say, enough is enough?

The child you coddle today, and placate with the toys of a sick society, will be the same child who will disrespect you, steal from you, and threaten your life tomorrow. And what will they teach their children? That presidents are liars? That teachers are perverts? That everyone does drugs or poses nude? That no one should expect to live to be thirty?

How about, it's okay to lie, cheat, and steal from the weak. It's okay to abuse yourself, as long as you aren't hurting others. Or maybe that it's okay to drop out and put your head in the sand, while the world around you comes tumbling down. Is this the legacy we are leaving our children? It sounds all too familiar. Every great nation that preceded us traveled the same path we are now on.

We are at a crossroads. The road we are traveling is a perilous one. We must choose whether to turn back onto the path of decency or to become more like those lurking in the bushes to ambush us and rob us of our dreams and our future. Remember, it makes little difference how good and moral you are. It won't matter which schools you send your children to and what grades they make. If we ignore the problems of our society, which persists in the permissiveness of unethical behavior, then we will guarantee the victimization of every decent person, by the growing number of social deviates we now inspire.

Someone must speak out. Alone he or she will be verbally crucified by the misguided liberalists. But if enough of us are left who care, if enough of us can still remember how it's suppose to be, rather than giving in to the way it is, then there's still hope.

It won't be easy to rebuild paradise, but it's worth a try. What have we got to lose that we are not already losing?

I wish we could see how truly beautiful this world could be, if we'd just make it so. I wish we could lay down our weapons in order to embrace a new tomorrow.

Before I die, I'd like to see just one week, where a moratorium was called on hatred, violence, and bigotry. Just one single week where the drug pushers and gang members would stop preying on the weak and the innocent. One single week where all of the nations of the world would stop fighting long enough to bask in the light of peace and brotherhood.

I know it sounds hopeless, but it's still my wish. Wish what *you* want. I firmly believe that forever can begin with just one week. I firmly believe that together we can build that world.

We don't *have* to do anything but die. But we've got eternity to be dead and only a moment to be alive. Let's make the most of our moment.

Good night, Pat. Pleasant dreams.

THE END

About the Author

Michael Andre McCoy was born in Fort Lee, Virginia, and raised in the San Fernando Valley, a suburb of Los Angeles, California. He attended Wayne State University in Detroit, Michigan, for two years, on a track scholarship, majoring in Political Science and minoring in Psychology. Upon returning to California, he resumed his stage performances of original poetry and musical compositions, as well as attending California State University at Northridge as a Philosophy major. Michael graduated with honors in 1981 from Morehouse College in Atlanta, Georgia, with a B.A. degree in Philosophy and a Music minor. He is currently pursuing a career as a songwriter/singer, and he has already composed the music for the movie based on this book.